TRACK OF A KILLER

TRACK OF A KILLER

by

Stephen Overholser

The Golden West Large Print Books
Long Preston, North Yorkshire,
BD23 4ND, England.

British Library Cataloguing in Publication Data.

Overholser, Stephen
    Track of a killer.

    A catalogue record of this book is
    available from the British Library

    ISBN   978-1-84262-918-5 pbk

First published 1982

Copyright © 1982 by Stephen Overholser

Cover illustration © Michael Thomas

The moral right of the author has been asserted

Published in Large Print 2012 by arrangement with
Golden West Literary Agency

The Golden West Large Print is an imprint of Library Magna
Books Ltd.

Printed and bound in Great Britain by
T.J. (International) Ltd., Cornwall, PL28 8RW

This book is dedicated to
Al and Mary McGowen
And to the memory of their son,
Chuck, never forgotten

CHAPTER 1

At dawn the train slowed before stopping alongside the water tower and loading platform in Yellow Pine, Montana. Clay Scarborough swung down from the passenger coach to the platform. Behind him came the Old Man, hobbling stiffly after the long ride from Chicago.

Clay paused while the Old Man caught up, then they walked side by side a short distance away from the hissing steam engine where Specs, a Circle R cowhand, and Junior, the young wrangler, held a dozen saddle horses and a black buggy for the Old Man.

'We lost some stock, Mr Rawls,' Junior called out the moment Clay and the Old Man were in earshot.

'What?' Jess Rawls demanded, scowling. 'Too damned early in the morning for that kind of talk.'

'We lost about fifty head out of the north pasture,' Junior said loudly, as though eager to deliver bad news.

Clay's nostrils filled with the stench of Junior's body odor. He was a scrawny kid with hips barely wide enough to hold up the heavy cartridge belt strapped around his waist. The old model Remington army revolver holstered on his right thigh, a foot long and weighing three pounds, looked too big for him.

'Tell him,' Junior urged the lanky cowhand beside him.

Specs adjusted the round, silver-rimmed spectacles on his long nose. 'Well, I was riding along the foothills, and I come onto fresh tracks in a mud bank. Three shod horses.' He paused. 'You and Clay and most of the hands was in Chicago ... so I knowed those tracks wasn't made by our riders–'

'When was this?' Rawls demanded.

'Oh ... day before yesterday,' Specs drawled with painful slowness. 'I follered the tracks 'til dark, and made camp. Rained in the night ... come morning I couldn't pick up the trail. But I could see that they run off a bunch from the north pasture.'

Rawls yanked the battered felt hat off his head and ran a hand through his white hair. Turning to his foreman, he said, 'Clay, get some grub at Mays's Store, and take a few hands with you to the north pasture. See what you can find.'

Clay nodded, and Rawls clapped the hat back on his head. Striding to his waiting horse, Clay was followed by Junior.

'I'll go with you, Clay.'

Throwing the stirrup over his saddle, Clay pulled the cinch tight. Ramrod of the Circle

R for the last five years, he was a lean, raw-boned man of twenty-nine with pale blue eyes, and now a day's growth of beard darkened his jaw. He'd already decided who would ride with him – Specs and two other top hands, Wash Stuart and Curly Baker.

Clay shook his head as he took the stirrup down.

'Damn!' Junior whispered harshly. 'How the hell am I supposed to get any experience if I stay on the home ranch all the time?' Rage hardened his face. Before Clay could reply, Junior turned away, his boots scuffing dirt with every angry step as he walked to the Old Man.

Clay had seen this look on the kid's face once before. Last time they'd argued over the same subject, they were alone in the Circle R horse barn. Junior had snatched out the big revolver the Old Man had given him and point it at Clay, thumbing back the hammer with a *click*. 'Put that thing away,' Clay had said, and after a tense moment Junior holstered the gun. But the look of hatred remained in his eyes.

Eager and dangerous, Clay had thought of him ever since. And it didn't help any that the Old Man had brought Junior to the ranch from Yellow Pine like a starving puppy, and told Clay to make a wrangler out of him.

With no experience and little talent for ranch work, the kid had trouble with every-

11

thing from wearing his spurs upside down to staying in the saddle of the gentlest mare in the corral. When he'd given his only name as Smith, the cowhands had tried out several first names on him, looking for one that fit – Smitty, Buster, Chip, Pistol, Junior. The last had stuck, and was intended with some sarcasm after the kid had revealed a hot temper and a tendency to complain.

Clay looked at the eleven Circle R cowhands straggling sleepily from the Great Northern train to their horses. The men wore high-heeled boots of stitched cowhide, denim or corduroy trousers, light-colored shirts under dark vests, and silk handkerchiefs loosely tied around their necks. High-crowned hats, many new, were cocked back on their heads, showing pale foreheads over tanned faces.

Most of the men had bruises and blackened eyes to show for their trip to Chicago. In the Union Stockyards the steers had been off-loaded, counted again, and sold at high market prices. Then came the celebration, which had been a matter of bunkhouse discussion and speculation since spring. In a series of big-city saloons expensive whiskey had been gulped down, 25-cent cigars smoked, brass-knuckled Chicagoans had been fought, and later the women in Sally's Palace had been humped.

Clay raised his voice to the approaching

men. 'Curly, Wash, I want you to ride with me. Specs, mount up and show us where you found those tracks.' He added, 'The rest of you can ride back to the ranch with Mr Rawls.'

'If you catch those thieving bastards,' the Old Man said as Clay swung up into the saddle, 'string them up to the nearest goddamn tree and leave them there.'

Casting a lopsided grin at his boss, Clay said, 'And after I'm convicted of murder, you'll bust me out of prison before I'm hauled off to the gallows, won't you, Jess?'

The Old man gave no response, but he jerked his head at the kid standing beside him. 'Take him with you, Clay.'

Clay's grin faded. 'We've got a long, hard ride in front of us–'

'Take him,' Rawls repeated.

Clay's jaw tightened. He was aware that all the cowhands were watching, and all the men knew what was happening. Clay was paid seventy-five dollars a month to run the Circle R, but at the same time he was paid to do what he was told.

Nodding once, Clay said, 'Let's ride.'

CHAPTER 2

Flanked by Junior and the three cowhands, Clay rode out of Yellow Pine, passing the loading pens and the dripping water tower where the train was stopped. The town was only two false-fronted buildings facing each other across the short, rutted street – Mays's General Store & Post Office and Frenchy's Bon Ton Saloon. Half a dozen log cabins were clustered around them.

Yellow Pine was dwarfed by the vast stretch of grasslands. From horizon to horizon this was cattle country – open range – and fifteen miles to the north Jess Rawls' Circle R Ranch sprawled out for thirty thousand deeded acres.

Sticking out of the northwestern horizon like the teeth of an upturned bucksaw was the Bear Paw mountain range. Clay glanced up at them and saw a white edge on the highest peaks. Winter would come from that direction.

Yellow Pine's street quickly dwindled to a set of wheel ruts in the grass. The ruts dipped down into Cottonwood Creek, and the five horses splashed across the shallow stream. On the far bank stood a low, windowless cabin with a sod roof. A railroader's lantern with a red chimney hung from the doorjamb. The establishment bore no sign, but was known throughout northern Montana as Dirty Gertie's.

As the riders drew even with the cabin, the plank door swung open. A fat woman, nearly as wide as the doorway, came out and beckoned to the cowhands. Long, stringy hair fell past her shoulders, and her pendulous breasts swung mightily under her thin white gown.

'Gertie's calling you, Wash,' Curly said.

'She wants *you*,' Wash replied as they rode past. 'You've always had a way with porkers.'

Clay glanced at the saddle partners who rawhided one another without cracking a smile. They were exact opposites in appearance. He wondered what mystery of friendship had drawn them together.

Wash was a big man, over six feet, with a thick neck and heavy muscles in his shoulders and upper arms. His first name was short for Washington. It was a name that was a mark of pride among slave parents claiming to have ancestors who had worked land owned by the nation's first President.

Curly, on the other hand, was small. He was as bald as an egg and as white and wore a long handlebar mustache. With a chip on his shoulder and a temper as short as the man, Curly often started Saturday-night brawls in Frenchy's Bon Ton Saloon with railroaders or cowhands from surrounding ranches. And Wash had to step in and finish them.

Curly's chin was purpled with a 'Chicago' bruise, and the knuckles of Wash's right hand were still swollen. Clay knew both men to be solid cowhands, though. They would give a day's work for a day's pay, and then some. Specs was the same. A man who might be judged stupid from the slow way he spoke, Specs could do any job on the ranch, from doctoring cows and horses to mending fences and building corrals.

Specs liked to save his money and had no interest in a trip to Chicago. Junior was always eager to go somewhere, but for some reason had wanted to stay behind and do his chores around the home ranch.

Clay noticed that Junior turned in his saddle and looked back at the beckoning Dirty Gertie. He kept looking until they topped a hill on the far side of Cottonwood Creek and rode out of sight.

All morning Clay pushed his gelding at a fast pace across the rolling grasslands, stopping only a few times to rest. A light, cold wind kicked up at midday, blowing from the mountains like a warning.

They halted and put on light coats that were tied behind their saddles, then ate a quick meal of sardines and cheese and crackers. Opening a can of peaches, they speared out the halves with their pocket knives, passed a pint of rye, and then rode on toward the mountains.

Clay saw that Junior was saddle-sore, grimacing as he rode. He held the saddle horn with his free hand, often standing in the stirrups. But at least he had not yet complained.

They reached the north pasture in the afternoon. Ringed by grassy hills on three sides, and the high Bear Paw mountains to the northwest, this huge pasture was used for summer grazing. Here Circle R stock had been gathered during fall roundup when the four-year-old steers were cut from the herd for shipment to the Chicago stockyards. A herd of young steers and heifers had been left behind.

Specs pointed to the dark mud bank along a tributary to Cottonwood Creek. It was there he had first picked up the tracks of three shod horses. Leading the way to the far edge of the pasture, Specs reined up and gestured toward the high mountains.

'Seemed like they was headed that way,' Specs drawled, 'but come morning I couldn't find their tracks, what with the rain and all.'

'Who the hell would drive stock up there?' Curly asked, squinting into the cold wind. 'The critters would be sore-footed in an hour.'

Clay looked up at the highest mountain, Squaw Peak. New snow speckled the granite face. 'I've got an idea,' he said.

The cowhands followed as Clay spurred his gelding to a faint Blackfoot Indian trail, unused for the many years since the tribes had been moved to reservations. It led over a natural pass on the south side of Squaw Peak, and on to Canada.

Half a mile away, on higher ground at the base of the peak, was a grassy flat. Surrounded by pine trees, this ground bore the signs of ancient campsites. Here, Clay had hunted elk and had picked up spear tips and arrowheads made of flint.

Iron horseshoes rang against the rocks as the men urged their mounts up the ridge toward the flat. Fresh cow droppings clung to sharp pieces of granite.

Clay reached the flat first, and the sight and stink of slaughter there made his horse shy and rear. The three cowhands and Junior moved up behind him. The men were silent for a long moment as they looked at the scene, then they swore in disgust.

The grassy flat was littered with the remains of thirty to forty young steers and heifers. The animals had been crudely butchered. Sledge-hammered heads, slashed hides, and gleaming entrails lay scattered across the ground. Some of the carrion had been picked and chewed by birds, wolves, and bears.

A sudden crashing sound from the stand of pines off to the left made Clay whirl in his saddle, draw his Colt .45, and fire at a flash of movement. The loud report reverberated off the towering mountain, making all the horses prance.

A brown donkey wandered out of the trees, ears cocked in the direction of the horsemen. Clay looked at the cowhands. Curly and Wash had drawn their revolvers and aimed at the donkey. A silent moment passed before they looked at one another and laughed softly. Junior stared at Clay in amazement at the quick draw.

'You missed him,' Curly said, holstering his gun, 'but you sure showed him who's boss.'

'Now I'm wondering who's the jackass,' Clay said. He shoved his revolver into the oiled holster on his hip. Even though he'd been certain the thieves were long gone, he was jumpy enough to shoot first and ask questions later.

'Get a rope on that critter,' Clay said. 'I want a closer look at him.'

Wash and Curly turned their horses and rode off in opposite directions, circling the donkey.

'What do you make of this?' Specs asked.

Clay glanced at the natural pass over the mountain. 'Three or four rustlers brought a string of pack animals on the old Blackfoot trail over Squaw Peak. They left the donkeys here and rode down to the north pasture where they rounded up as much stock as they could handle. They drove them up here and did a quiet butchering job, loaded the meat on their donkeys, and packed over the mountain the way they had come.'

Specs nodded. 'And right now they're selling steaks to the goldminers over there.'

'That's right,' Clay said. 'With winter coming to the gold district, those rustlers can just about name their price. No hungry miner is going to ask for a bill of sale, either.'

Junior listened intently to Clay's explanation, and looked at the faint trail Clay had pointed out.

Wash did the hazing, and Curly dropped a loop over the donkey's head. On the animal's back were scars from a pack saddle. The cowhands brought the donkey to Clay.

'Looks like H-T,' Clay said, leaning over in his saddle while he rubbed hair back from the brand on the donkey's flank. 'Ever see that one in a brand book?'

The cowhands shook their heads.

A gust of icy wind swept off the mountain top. Clay straightened in the saddle and gave his Stetson a tug. He glanced up at the gray sky. The wind carried a swirl of snowflakes now.

'Well, let's take this jackass back to the

home ranch,' Clay said. 'I don't look forward to telling the Old Man about this, but at least we won't be empty-handed.'

CHAPTER 3

After nightfall the riders topped a ridge overlooking the home ranch in the long valley below. The light of half a moon seeped through scudding clouds, and the buildings of the Circle R Ranch made an eerie sight. Lamps in the main house and nearby bunkhouse glowed through small windows like the unblinking eyes of nocturnal beasts.

Beyond those squat buildings loomed a log horse barn and the small cabin Clay shared with the ranch cook. Behind them was a grove of cottonwood trees along the creek. As Clay led the way downslope, he heard dry leaves clattering with the wind.

After tending their horses and turning the donkey into a corral, the tired men went into the main house. They entered through a side door by a wood pile, into the messhall and kitchen. Clay led the way as the men trooped in with a stomping of boots and ringing of spurs, slapping hands together that were numbed by cold.

Cookie, the barrel-bellied ranch cook with

a walrus mustache under his pocked nose, had been expecting them. Coffee steamed from a pot on the stove, and beef stew and sourdough bread warmed in the oven.

Cookie was a slow-moving, taciturn man in his sixties who wore the garb of a cow-hand, including boots with run-over heels. A lifetime on horseback had left him too stove-up to ride, but he had never given up his old clothes, a favorite vest, or even the battered saddle at the head of his bunk. He cooked for the crew, not because he liked the work, but because he was determined to keep a place, a position, on the ranch.

'Rawls is waiting for you,' Cookie said.

Clay nodded while he poured a mug of coffee, added a shot of sweetened condensed milk, and then passed behind the men at the mess table who silently awaited supper. He stepped through a low doorway into the main room of the ranch house, where a fire blazed in the stone fireplace.

Clay strode to it and stood on the grizzly-bear rug, turning his back to the leaping flames. Suspended on a length of wire from the ceiling was a lantern that cast pale light on the four log walls of the room. Chairs built of deer antlers and carved pine limbs were scattered around. The pieces of furn-iture were the work of countless winter days when the home ranch crew was snowed in.

'Jess,' Clay called in the direction of an

open doorway to his right.

'Clay? That you?'

'Yeah.' Clay sipped hot coffee from the mug, then turned to face the Old Man who walked stiff-legged out of his bedroom, shouldering into his suspenders.

'Turn up anything?' Rawls asked. His thin white hair stood on end, and a pink crease ran down the side of his face where he'd slept.

Clay told him of the pole-axed steers and heifers and described the remains he'd found on the flat above the north pasture. He advanced his theory about the rustlers.

Rawls nodded agreement. He stared into the fire and said, 'I wisht gold had never been found in the Bear Paws.'

'The rustlers lost a pack mule,' Clay said, 'branded H-T. In the morning I'll wire a report to the Stockgrowers Association. Maybe we can get some help in tracing the brand.'

Rawls shrugged, peering absently into the red-orange flames that licked at blackened pine logs.

Clay had expected the Old Man to be enraged, demanding that armed riders be sent out after the thieves. And Clay already had his reply ready: The trail was too cold for pursuit and a storm was coming. All they could do now was send for the county sheriff and deputies.

But instead of exploding, the Old Man simply turned to Clay and thrust his thumbs through his suspenders.

'We've got work to do around here, Clay,' he said, 'a pile of it.'

'True enough,' Clay said, watching his lined face for a clue to his meaning.

Rawls looked around the room with a critical eye. 'We've got to fix this place up, add a room.'

'Add a room?' Clay repeated. Plenty of jobs needed to be done before winter set in, from rebuilding the drift fence along the south boundary of Circle R range to laying in a supply of firewood and coal to chinking log walls against frigid winds. But adding a room was one job that had never occurred to him.

Rawls moved across the room to a crude table under an elk head mounted on the wall. The table served as the Old Man's desk, and was piled high with papers and ledger books. As far as Clay knew, these had been accumulating ever since Rawls had felled trees by himself and built this log house thirty years ago.

The Old Man lifted a sheet of paper off the top of the heap and brought it to Clay. 'Telegram's from Baltimore,' he said in a voice that quavered with excitement. 'I picked it up in town this morning. My sister's granddaughter is coming out for Christmas. Clay, we've got to get this old place fixed up, get a shine on it for a proper lady.'

Clay looked up from the telegraphed message, too amazed to speak.

'Don't tell any of the hands about Annie coming out here,' Rawls said in a low voice. 'When I want 'em to know, I'll tell 'em.'

In the cool darkness of his cabin Clay lay in his bunk and listened to Cookie's rhythmic snoring. He thought about a young woman being on the ranch. The idea was hard to accept. A man's place, that's what the Circle R had always been.

Clay's thoughts turned to the Old Man. That nickname was used beyond Rawls' hearing by all the Circle R hands and half the people in Montana. It was respectfully meant.

Rawls was a wiry man who'd been tough as a spike in his day. He'd carved a cattle ranch out of wilderness at a time when Indians still believed they had the run of the land. Rawls had made peace with the Blackfeet by letting them cross Circle R range to their hunting grounds in the Bear Paw mountains, and insured that peace by not riding after them every time they ran off a few head of cattle for food.

As much as Clay respected Jess Rawls, he knew the Old Man was becoming more contrary and unpredictable every year. Rawls frequently said he wanted Clay to ramrod the outfit, but at the same time he refused to let him really take over. The Old Man moved cattle from one pasture to another, bought and sold horses and bulls, and hired and fired on a whim, all behind Clay's back. And a day later he was likely to forget what he'd done.

Trying to hold the ranch together through all this uncertainty, Clay often humored the Old Man with wisecracks, hoping he would see his own foolishness. Sometimes the trick worked, sometimes it didn't. This morning when Rawls had ordered him to lynch the cattle rustlers, Clay tried to make a joke of it. This was 1894, not the '70s, and Clay hoped he'd reminded Rawls that times had changed.

In the morning after breakfast Clay met the cowhands at the horse corral adjoining the log barn and gave the men their assignments. The night wind had swept the snow away and left a clear sky at sunrise. The crisp, still air of early morning was the surest sign yet of a fast approaching winter.

Clay sent a crew of four to start work on repairing the wire drift fence. That fence marked the south boundary of the Circle R, and prevented the cattle from being wind-driven far to the south during winter storms. Without it, the Circle R's spring roundup would have to be held in Amarillo.

Clay gave Specs another crew to take axes

and saws and a flatbed wagon to the pine forest at the base of the Bar Paw mountains. The men would drop trees selected by Specs, trim them, and haul a load of logs back to the home ranch. Then the same crew would bring in more logs for firewood, cut them into eighteen-inch lengths, and split them.

Besides being a cowhand, Specs was a fair logger and a very good carpenter. He was in charge of building the addition to the ranch house. The other hands did not know it, but Specs would be paid extra for this job. He had already agreed to stay on for the winter, confiding to Clay that he expected to have enough money saved within two years to buy his own ranch.

Clay sent the rest of the men out on the range to tend stock. One crew, including Curly and Wash, were sent to the north pasture. There they would comb the hills for cattle and drive any young steers and heifers they found to winter pasture on the south sector of the ranch.

Clay warned all the men to be on the lookout for strangers, and to bring in anyone who couldn't give a good reason for being on Circle R land.

Junior sat on the top pole of the corral, sullenly watching. When Specs brought the flatbed wagon, Junior asked loudly, 'What in hell's the Old Man adding a room to the house for?'

Clay did not reply. He knew the question was in the minds of all the cowhands, but the men knew it was not their business to ask.

After a silent moment, Curly said, 'The Old Man probably figures the wrangler needs his own bedroom.'

Junior shot an angry look at Curly as the men chuckled and moved to their horses. Taking reins in hand, they swung up into their saddles. The spirited cow ponies bucked and sunfished. The riders worked the morning kinks out, swearing all the while. After they rode off in their separate directions, Clay caught and saddled his big gelding.

'I should be riding with one of those crews,' Junior said.

'You will after you've had some experience–' Clay began.

Junior jumped down from the corral and faced Clay, his fists clenched, legs spread wide. 'Hell, that's the problem. You won't let me get any experience.'

'You'll learn by wrangling horses–'

'I've been through this with you before,' Junior interrupted. 'You can't get it through your head. Things are going to be different after today. I'm going to the Old Man. You'll have to get someone else to shovel manure around here.'

Junior turned abruptly and walked away from the corral to the ranch house. Clay watched him go, debating whether to follow or not.

The kid strode across the porch and threw the door open. Seeing that he'd entered the house without bothering to close the door, Clay decided to give the kid some time to cool off. He mounted his horse and rode to Yellow Pine.

CHAPTER 4

The telegraph office was a small, unpainted clapboard building on the railroad-loading platform, where the Great Northern tracks marked the end of Yellow Pine's street.

Smoke drifted out of the stovepipe on the building. Clay tied his horse at the rail and went in. He found the telegrapher, Henry Reid, hunched over the warmth of a pot-belly stove. The cramped office smelled of coal smoke.

'Morning, Henry,' Clay said, closing the door behind him.

Reid straightened up. He was a thin, pasty man who wore several years of clothing and a black wool cap pulled over his ears. 'Well, well, Clay, what brings you back to town so soon?'

'I need to send a wire to the Stockgrowers

Association,' Clay replied. He added, 'And the county sheriff. Got a little problem.'

Reid slid his swivel chair to a desk and shoved a pad of paper and stubby pencil across it. 'Write your message, and I'll send her. The line's clear.'

While Clay wrote the two messages, Reid asked, 'Heard the big news?'

Clay did not reply until he'd finished writing. He read through both messages, then handed the pad of paper back to the telegrapher. 'What news is that?'

The moment their eyes met, Clay realized the two of them shared a secret. Reid had received the telegraphed message from Annie, and was one of three men in Montana who knew she was coming.

Although Reid was bound by an oath of secrecy, Clay wondered if he had ever let anything important slip. The man had an ear, literally, to nearly everything that went on in these parts.

'A big mining outfit's coming to Yellow Pine,' Reid said, his eyes narrowing. 'Majestic Mining and Milling. They're going to build a big warehouse here in town, and the rumor is that they'll run a spur off this rail line to the gold district in the Bear Paws.'

'I've heard a lot of rumors about mining,' Clay said, smiling.

'Yeah, but this one makes good sense,' Reid said. 'I know for a fact Majestic has bought up most of a mountain in the gold district, and they can run rails to it from here by cutting south of Squaw Peak.'

Clay considered that notion. 'I reckon they can.'

Reid glanced at the Great Northern calendar hanging on the plank wall over his desk. 'In four, no, five days Majestic is sending two carloads of supplies and building material. And a crew is coming all the way from Chicago to start construction on the warehouse.'

'They'd better build fast,' Clay said. 'Snow's coming.'

'They'll get the rough work done,' Reid said knowingly as he leaned back in his chair, 'and finish up in the spring.' He paused. 'You know, Clay, you ought to buy some land here in town. As an investment, I mean.'

Clay grinned crookedly and shook his head.

'It's better than keeping your wages locked in Frenchy's safe,' Reid said.

'I don't have to worry about my bar bill that way,' Clay replied.

'I'm serious,' Reid said with a trace of irritation. 'I'm talking about investing your money. I've bought some town lots myself. So has Al Mays. We'll double our money next spring when land speculators get wind of Majestic's plans.'

'Thanks for the tip,' Clay said. 'I'll think

on it.' He glanced toward the messages he'd written to remind Reid why he was there.

Reid came down in his chair, turned to his telegraph key, and tapped out one message to the Montana Stockgrowers Association and the second one to the county sheriff.

Outside, Clay untied his horse and led the animal across the rutted street past Mays's General Store to Frenchy's Bon Ton Saloon. The building was a log cabin with a plank false front facing the street. This time of day the interior was dark and silent, smelling strongly of spilled whiskey and stale smoke.

Clay walked in, stopping for a moment while his eyes adjusted to the gloom. A long bar with a brass foot rail ran along one side of the room. On the other side were round tables and captain's chairs amid brass spittoons. The floor was dirt, packed hard.

'Frenchy?' Clay said.

Pale light filtered into the saloon when the rear door swung open. Frenchy lived in a small back room with a bunk, a sheet-iron cook stove, and an enormous steel safe with two combination locks.

'Closed,' Frenchy said, leaning out of the doorway. In his right hand was a short-barreled pistol.

'I came to make a deposit, Frenchy,' Clay said.

'Clay!' he shouted, moving out of the doorway and walking rapidly toward him. 'I did not recognize you. Forgive me!'

Clay grinned as he watched the slender man thrust the pistol into his waistband. Frenchy was always neatly attired, something of a dandy, and he was exuberantly friendly to those he liked. Clay had laid his gunbarrel over the head of more than one trouble-maker in this saloon, and for that Frenchy liked him very much.

'You return from Chicago yesterday,' Frenchy said. 'I see you ride past.'

Clay nodded. 'I got home with some money.'

'You may be the only Circle R man who did!' Frenchy exclaimed. His small pointed beard twitched as he spoke making him appear more excitable than he was.

In many ways, Frenchy was a mysterious man. He seemed open and friendly, yet he never spoke of his past, not even in casual conversation. Perhaps because of this a number of stories about him circulated.

Clay had heard that the man had come to America with a fortune, but either he had lost it foolishly or it had been stolen from him. Clay had also heard that Frenchy had murdered a woman in New Orleans, sought a remote place to hide, and found it when he arrived in Yellow Pine by train a dozen years ago.

Despite the rumors, Clay had never heard anyone challenge Frenchy's honesty. His steel safe was the nearest thing to a bank in these parts, and cowhands and ranchers alike kept their savings in it.

Clay opened his shirt down to his waist and brought out a money belt. He counted out three hundred dollars and handed the greenbacks to the saloonkeeper.

'I bring you a receipt,' Frenchy said, retreating quickly to the back room.

'Give me a count, will you, Frenchy?'

'Yes, yes, one moment,' he replied over his shoulder. Closing the door of the back room, he loudly shoved the deadbolt home.

When Frenchy returned he handed Clay a receipt and said, 'You have $1,852 in my safe. You wish to count it?'

Clay shook his head and pocketed the receipt. The sum didn't seem much for five years' work.

'I see that kid, Junior, still works for the Circle R,' Frenchy said.

'The Old Man's taken him under his wing,' Clay said.

Frenchy pursed his lips. 'You tell Mr Rawls to watch out for that kid. He's a mean one, mean as a dog in a corner. Tell Mr Rawls I say so.'

'All right,' Clay said, studying the Frenchman.

'The kid came to me after he was booted off a Great Northern freight,' Frenchy said. 'I gave him work here as a swamper. After one week, I catch him stealing whiskey one day, cash out of my coin box the next.' He added, 'But more than a thief, Clay, he's mean. Tell Mr Rawls I say so.'

'Clay nodded. 'I'll tell him.' Before leaving the Bon Ton Saloon, Clay asked, 'What do you make of this mining talk, Frenchy?'

He shrugged, turning his small hands up at his sides. 'Talk, talk. I hear such talk every night in here.'

'Yellow Pine will change plenty when that Majestic outfit moves in,' Clay said.

Frenchy shrugged again. 'More customers, no? I sell beer and whiskey until I make my fortune. Then I do nothing that doesn't please me.'

Clay grinned. The American Dream summed up by a Frenchman, he thought.

Riding back to the home ranch, Clay considered Henry Reid's advice. Maybe the telegrapher would double his money come spring. Then again, he might be saddled with lots in a place that never would be a real town.

To hell with speculating, Clay thought, spurring his horse along the wheel ruts in the high grass. He had come by his money the hard way, at seventy-five dollars a month plus a bonus after every trip to the Chicago stockyards when the Circle R turned a profit. And every year since Clay first took over as ramrod on the Old Man's ranch, the herd of cattle had grown and the profits from the sale of steers in the fall had increased.

Clay thought, *When the time comes to buy a piece of land, I'm not going to sink my money into a town lot. I'll pick up a little ranch somewhere and own it forever.*

This was his dream of the future, a vague picture of a ranch near the mountains with plenty of grass and trees and a creek meandering past a small ranch house. Included in this dream was a woman he had married, and the family they were raising together.

But as Clay rode on toward the home ranch, another vision came to his mind. This one was immediate and not so vague. If a gold boom brought prosperity to Yellow Pine, it would also bring problems to the Circle R, from more rustling to a rush of prospectors seeking their fortunes.

CHAPTER 5

From the runway of the house barn Clay looked outside and saw Curly and Wash herd a lame bull in from the bull pasture. They hazed the big animal into an empty corral, roped his head and hind legs, and threw him.

Junior rode behind them, gripping his saddle horn with both hands. The Circle R mare he'd ridden that day wandered to the corral and stopped.

The bull had foot-rot disease, an ailment the cowhands called 'mud fever,' and the critter's legs were swollen. While Junior looked on, Curly and Wash bent over the bull and sawed a lariat vigorously between the cleft of each hoof. The swelling burst, and pus ran out. Then Wash dipped a brush into a can of turpentine and swabbed the wounds.

The bull bellowed and tossed his head, scraping a groove deep into the ground with his down horn. The animal had been in pain before, but now he was in agony.

Clay saw what was happening too late to stop it. He strode from the barn toward the corral, seeing Junior inside it with Curly. Wash had already retreated and climbed through the fence and now Curly suddenly shook the ropes loose and dove out of the corral. The bull practically exploded to his feet, bellowing with rage.

Junior stood frozen, staring at the bull, as though disbelieving that an animal so large could move with such grace and speed. The bull faced Junior and pawed the earth, throwing great clods of dirt and manure in high arcs behind him. Then he lowered his head and charged.

Junior came unglued and threw himself to

one side, skidding on his face as the bull thundered past. Rising to his hands and knees, Junior watched wide-eyed as the bull quickly turned and again lowered his head and came roaring back.

Clay ran to the corral in time to see Junior dive away, the bull's slashing horn missing him by inches. Junior rolled, hitting a post of the corral fence. He lay still, and the bull came for him again.

Clay reached Junior and pulled him under the bottom pole of the fence just as the bull struck it with his head. Clay helped the kid to his feet and steadied him.

Junior yanked away from Clay, his face stained with mud and manure and tears. 'Curly, I'm calling you out!'

Curly moved around the circle of the corral fence and faced Junior a dozen paces away. 'I told you to do everything I did, didn't I?'

'You never told me...' Junior fought through his anger for words, and finally sputtered, 'Hell with it!' His right hand swept to the holster on his hip.

Curly laughed.

Junior grabbed a handful of air. He looked in surprise down at his empty holster, then his gaze shot out to the corral. There in the dirt lay the army revolver, and the bull stood over it, sniffing the weapon.

'I'll wait here while you go get your

mankiller,' Curly said.

As enraged as the bull had been, Junior suddenly charged Curly, lashing out with both fists. Curly smoothly sidestepped, and slugged him on the side of his jaw as he stumbled past.

Junior lost his balance and sprawled to the ground, but got back to his feet and turned, fists raised, advancing cautiously this time. The moment Junior moved into Curly's practiced range, he was hit again with a right fist, and then a left, the punches landing flat and hard on the kid's face.

Clay heard the sounds of fists striking flesh, and he saw Junior's knees buckle. 'That's enough.'

Breathing hard, Junior said, 'I'll kill the bas–'

Curly stepped in and swung a looping right that hit Junior in front of his ear. The kid's eyes rolled, and he staggered on weak knees.

'That's enough, I said,' Clay ordered, stepping between them. He faced Junior. 'Take your horse to the barn. Go on!'

Junior's face was red where he'd been hit. He lowered his fists slowly, glowering first at Curly, then at Clay. After a moment he moved away and went to his mare.

Curly examined the knuckles of his right hand. 'You should have let me finish the job, Clay. That kid needs his clock cleaned worse

39

than anybody I ever saw.'

'You're right about that,' Clay said. 'But you know how the Old Man feels about fighting.'

'I know how he is about that worthless kid,' Curly said. 'I wish I'd never let the Old Man talk us into letting him ride with us. The kid tells the Old Man he wants to learn ranch work, but he don't listen to what us cowhands tell him. All that kid's got is a smart mouth.'

Clay glanced at Wash and saw the man give an exasperated nod of agreement.

'Give the kid to someone else tomorrow, Clay,' Wash said. 'One day with him is enough.'

After supper Clay went into the bunkhouse. The building was long and low. It was built of logs and had a dirt roof. Potbelly stoves stood at either end and bunks lined the two longest walls. The cowhands who had been on the Circle R the longest had earned the bunks nearest the stoves.

Most of the men lay on their bunks, dozing or reading copies of the *Police Gazette*. The rest were gathered around one of the warm stoves, seated on upturned wooden boxes and nail kegs. A faded sign tacked on the wall read: No Drinking No Gambling Means No Fighting.

Clay found Curly and Wash at the far end of the smoky room. They were looking through a new J.C. Hyer Boot Catalogue. The men seated around the nearby stove were engaged in an argument over the trial of a French captain of artillery, Alfred Dreyfus, in Paris. The cowhands had brought home a Chicago weekly that published a long account of the trial and the background of the case, and now the bunkhouse lawyers passionately debated the man's guilt or innocence.

'The Old Man wants to see you, Curly,' Clay said.

The men seated around the stove fell silent, turning to see what would happen.

Curly looked up from the thick catalogue and grinned. 'Should I pack my war bag?'

'Not yet,' Clay said, trying to match the cowhand's easy smile.

Curly jerked his head toward the men who had been arguing the cause of justice in the Dreyfus case in Paris, France. 'I ain't much on defending myself, Clay. I'd just as soon pack my war bag and ride.'

'I know,' Clay said. 'But I'd like to go with you and hear what the Old Man has to say.' He glanced at Wash who looked on stoically.

Curly paused, then stood and picked up his sweat-rimmed Stetson. 'Take me to the guillotine.'

The blazing fireplace in the ranch house cast dancing shadows across the room. Clay found Rawls seated in a chair made of elk antlers bound together with tightened strips of leather.

'The wrangler tells me you handed him a whipping today,' Rawls said, looking up at Curly.

Upon entering the room Curly had taken off his hat. Now he held it in both hands before him, slowly turning it and sliding his callused hands along the curled brim. 'Yep,' he said.

'Junior tells me you suckered him into the corral,' Rawls went on, 'and turned a bull loose on him. That right?'

'That's about it,' Curly said, meeting the Old Man's steady gaze.

'You're through,' Rawls said. 'I don't allow fighting, and you know it.' He held out a strip of paper bearing figures and his signature. 'I've figured your wages. Cash this at Frenchy's.'

Curly moved a step forward and took the check from Rawls's hand.

'Now, hold on, Jess,' Clay said. 'The kid went after Curly. I saw him. Curly popped him a few times, and he could have hurt him worse.'

Rawls turned to his foreman. 'And you could have stopped it altogether, I'll wager.'

'You got that wrong, Mr Rawls,' Curly said. 'Clay stopped the kid as soon as he could. That damned Junior had blood in his eye.'

42

'You men keep playing pranks on him, that's why,' Rawls said, his voice thickening with emotion. 'And that's why he moved out of the bunkhouse to the horse barn.'

'Oh, hell, Mr Rawls,' Curly said, 'the kid left the bunkhouse because he won't take baths. He stinks something fierce. We thronged him in the trough more than once. Didn't do no good.'

'He'd learn ranch ways,' Rawls said, 'if you men would give him a chance.'

'The hell,' Curly said. 'He don't work much. Clay does most of the wrangling.'

'I don't hear my foreman complaining,' Rawls said, glancing at Clay, 'but I have heard enough out of you.'

'Suits me,' Curly said. He turned and walked out of the room, slapping his hat against his thigh.

'You just lost a top hand, Jess,' Clay said angrily, 'and another will go with him when he rides out.'

'It's time we trimmed the crew, anyhow,' Rawls said.

Clay shook his head. 'Not this way, Jess.'

'The hands are gonna have to learn to give Junior some slack,' Rawls said. 'He needs time to grow, that's all.'

Clay shook his head again. 'When you first brought the kid in, Jess, every man in the bunkhouse gave him a fair shake, tried to teach him the things he needs to know about working with horses and cattle. But Junior gave the men reason to dislike him. And now when you send him out with the cowhands, the men don't like it one bit–'

'He's just a kid finding his way,' Rawls interrupted.

'No,' Clay said. 'Curly told you Junior had blood in his eye. I've seen the same thing in him. He pulled that old army revolver on me once. And when I was in town, Frenchy told me to warn you about him. Frenchy said the kid's mean – mean as a cornered dog.'

The Old Man looked away, staring into the fire. Clay knew this conversation was over, that Rawls would not listen.

Old and losing his grip, Clay thought. No amount of talking would change that. He looked down at the Old Man's white head for a long moment, then left the room.

At dawn Clay heard horses outside. He quickly dressed, pulling on boots stiffened with cold, and left the cabin in time to see Curly and Wash ride out of the horse barn. Their canvas war bags were tied on the pair of spare horses they led, and clouds of steam gusted out of the animals' nostrils.

Clay strode across the yard to them. 'Sorry to see it end up this way, Curly. The Old Man's dead wrong. Wish I could make him see that.'

Curly nodded in reply, then said, 'Time

for us to ride out, anyway. Me and Wash are headed for Arizona.'

Clay reached up and shook hands with him, then he shook Wash's big hand. 'I hear the women down there believe ugly cowhands are for marrying. You two had better watch out.'

Wash chuckled, and a smile crept into Curly's face, raising his handlebar mustache slightly.

'Say,' Curly said, glancing toward the ranch house, 'just what the hell is the Old Man going to do with that extra room?'

Clay knew this question was on the mind of every cowhand in the bunkhouse and that various theories were circulating.

'A relative from back East is coming out here,' Clay said.

After a thoughtful pause, Wash smiled. 'I get it – the female kind.'

Clay nodded.

'Oh, hell,' Curly said, laughing. 'You'd better ride out with us, Clay. The Circle R ain't going to be a fit place for cowhand or cow critter this winter.'

CHAPTER 6

'You're going to have to make up your mind,' Clay said. 'Either you do the chores around here, or you saddle that mare and ride out with one of the crews.'

Junior stared down at the ground between them, arms folded across his chest against the cold. 'The Old Man told me–'

'I run this outfit, Junior,' Clay said. 'Everyone works around here. No exceptions.' Junior had gone over his head twice, and Clay knew he couldn't let it happen again.

Junior had been eager to gain the status of a working cowhand. But as the weather grew colder his enchantment with a carefree life on horseback faded into complaints about stubborn horses, stupid cows, and Montana ranch life in general.

Junior looked up, glowering at Clay. In a low voice, he said, 'I'll work around here today.'

'The horse barn needs shoveling out,' Clay said, turning and walking away.

The last of the Circle R stock was being drifted onto winter range as the season quickly changed. Winter here was an uncertain time of year, a long season when fierce, frigid storms howled out of the north country. These raging storms were abruptly punctuated by cold, diamond-clear days when Jess Rawls liked to say that a man could see all the way into tomorrow.

Cold winds now regularly brought gray clouds sweeping overhead like shredded canvas. The cowhands braced themselves against the stinging chill with bandanna handkerchiefs tied around their ears, muttering about packing their war bags and heading south where fruit grew on trees, not in a can.

Clay heard rumbling complaints from every crew. More than just the foul weather, not a man among them liked digging post holes or stringing and stapling wire fences or cutting firewood or any other job that couldn't be done on horseback.

Clay hired his winter crew from those men who did not complain but worked in stubborn silence. These were half a dozen top hands who would pair off and rotate between the home ranch and the two outlying line shacks through the dark weeks of winter. The remaining hands, men who lived from month to month on Circle R paychecks, would stick long enough to accumulate pocket money, then pack up and ride south with a horse or two trailing behind.

In the last days of autumn the addition to the ranch house quickly took shape once the logs were hauled in from the Bear Paw mountains. Specs measured and carefully notched each log with a hand axe, stacking them at right angles and chinking the gaps. Within a short time a log box was added to the south side of the house. Then, cutting a rectangle through the old weather logs, Specs fashioned a doorway to the new room.

Lumber had been ordered, and it arrived by rail in time for Specs to nail on a new shake roof before the first snowfall. After that he laid in plank flooring.

Arriving by Great Northern freight ten days later was a cast-iron parlor stove for this room, along with an odd assortment of womanly furnishings the Old Man had ordered from two dog-eared catalogues from Sears & Sawbuck and Monkey Wards.

Specs and his crew traveled to Yellow Pine to pick up these shipments, and from them Clay heard about the Majestic Mining & Milling construction crew now working there. He also learned that a message awaited him at the telegraph office.

Clay rode to town and saw four rail cars on the siding by the stick-loading pens. Two were living quarters for the workers and the other two were boxcars loaded with stone blocks and construction materials.

At the end of the street Clay saw eight or ten workers clearing ground for a founda-tion on the opposite end of the railroad platform from the telegraph office.

Tying his horse at the rail, Clay stepped onto the platform. He heard the clanging of shovels and repeated *thunks* of picks biting into the earth. The only member of this crew who wasn't on the business end of a tool was a squat, square-faced man wearing overalls and a knit cap with a short bill.

Tough as a harness bull, Clay thought, sizing him up as the foreman. Walking the length of the loading platform to the burly figure, Clay held out his hand to shake.

'I'm Clay Scarborough, of the Circle R ranch.'

'Angus Macdougal,' the man replied, grasping Clay's hand and giving it a hard pump.

'Putting up a warehouse, I hear,' Clay said.

Macdougal nodded grimly. 'I've got orders to lay in a foundation before the snow flies.'

Clay heard a Scottish burr in the man's deep voice. As their eyes met, Clay nodded and said, 'You've got your work cut out for you.'

'The bastards sitting in their warm offices back in Chicago give the orders, but they don't come out here to see what we're up against.' Macdougal exhaled loudly. 'Crew's getting edgy about the cold weather and being snowed in. T'other day some of the men got drunk in Frenchy's, and decided they could walk back home by following the rails. Had to fight them.' He pulled a pigskin glove off his hand to show darkly bruised knuckles.

Clay had sensed immediately that Macdougal was a foreman who ruled by brute strength. Now his back was against the wall about keeping his workers.

'You're not likely to get snowed in this early,' Clay said. 'But the cold is coming.'

'Damned if it ain't already got here,' Macdougal said humorlessly.

Clay strode back along the platform to the telegraph office. Inside, Henry Reid looked up at him over a tin cup of steaming, fragrant coffee.

'Majestic's here,' Reid said, setting the cup down on his desk. 'What'd I tell you? This little burg is off and running!'

Clay heard a falsely triumphant note in the telegrapher's voice, as though Reid was trying to convince himself, too.

'So I see,' Clay said. 'Is my wire here?'

Reid pushed his swivel chair back to the wall and without looking he reached up to a board with an envelope clipped to it. He pulled the envelope down and handed it to Clay.

Removing a sheet of paper from it, Clay unfolded it and read the message from the Montana Stockgrowers Association. The words were hand printed in large block letters:

CLAY SCARBOROUGH, FOREMAN
CIRCLE R RANCH
YELLOW PINE, MONTANA
H BAR T BRAND REGISTERED TO F.W.
MANCHESTER, ANTELOPE, WYOMING.
PACK ANIMALS REPORTED STOLEN
8/22/94. CATTLE RUSTLERS KNOWN TO BE
RAIDING HERDS WITHIN 100 MILE
RADIUS OF GOLD DISTRICT IN BEAR PAW
MOUNTAINS. PLEASE REPORT FURTHER
THEFTS OR SIGHTINGS OF SUSPECTED
RUSTLERS. ASSOCIATION IS CURRENTLY
WORKING WITH SHERIFF IN YOUR
COUNTY.

'Sending a reply?' Reid asked.

Clay shook his head. 'No, I reckon not.'

'Surveyors were here the other day,' Reid said. 'Came in a special Great Northern car. Brought maps and transits, and laid out a townsite.' He added, 'If you're going to buy lots, you'd better not wait.'

'I appreciate the advice,' Clay said.

Reid studied him. 'But you aren't going to take it, are you?'

'When it comes to land,' Clay said, 'I'm not much of a gambler. I gamble every day on cattle and weather.'

'This isn't a gamble,' Reid said, exasperated. 'I even borrowed cash to buy some more town lots.'

Clay smiled. 'Debts keep me awake at night, Henry.'

Reid shrugged indifferently and turned away. 'A man doesn't need a crystal ball to see what's happening here.'

Raw weather forced the Circle R crews to work at a rapid pace. By the time the last cowhand who'd not been hired to be part of the winter crew drew his pay and rode out, much had been done. The drift fence had been repaired, the addition to the ranch house was completed, and dozens of cords of split pine were piled against the kitchen and south wall of the bunkhouse.

A Lazy T rider passing by brought word that a message for the Old Man had arrived at the telegraph office. Rawls yelled for Junior to hitch up the horse to his buggy, and the two of them made a fast trip to Yellow Pine.

When they returned, Rawls ordered Clay to call a meeting of the cowhands, Specs, and Cookie. The men gathered in the main room of the ranch house and stood before the Old Man, hats in their hands, silent except for an occasional ringing of spur rowels when one of the cowhands shifted his feet.

'My sister's granddaughter, Annie, is coming sooner than I figured,' Rawls said, as though her arrival at the Circle R was common knowledge. 'In fact, she's on her way.'

Clay saw the men exchanging surprised glances, all but Junior.

'Just so we'll understand each other,' Rawls went on, 'I'll tell you right now what I expect from you men. Annie likes horses, and if she has any questions, I want you to answer them. If she needs help with anything, stop what you're doing and give her a hand. I expect you to be friendly to the girl, but not too friendly. Any man who bothers her is through on the Circle R. Remember that.'

Rawls paused. 'And I don't want to hear any loud cussing around here. Next time you get kicked or thronged, keep those words to yourself. Be careful where you spit, too.' He added, 'No more bathing in the crick. Lug water from the crick and use that old tub in the bunkhouse from now on.'

The cowhands listened in silence, nodding that they understood when the Old Man challenged them to either abide or ride.

Clay looked at Junior leaning against the mantel of the fireplace. A knowing smirk was on his face. Lately the kid had been helping clean up the ranch house and arranging the new furniture in Annie's room. Now Clay realized from his know-it-all expression that he'd been let in on The Secret some time ago.

The kid's expression told Clay something else, too, and a faint hope disappeared from his mind. Junior would not be driven off the Circle R by either the threat of hard work or the frigid winds of the approaching winter.

CHAPTER 7

Clay was reminded of a kitten the first time he saw Annie. Arriving at the ranch with the Old Man in the buggy, she climbed down and looked around uncertainly, as though overwhelmed by the open space of Montana. Her green eyes slowly blinked, and with her upturned nose and small heart-shaped mouth, Clay thought of a sleek kitten away from its mother for the first time.

'Clay, I'd like you to meet Annie Davenport, all the way from Baltimore, Maryland.' Rawls smiled broadly as he turned to her. 'This here's my ranch foreman, Clay Scarborough.'

Pulling the Stetson off his head, Clay said, 'Welcome to the Circle R, Annie.'

She looked up into his eyes and smiled shyly. 'Thank you Mr Scarborough. I'm glad to be out here.'

She wore a long wool skirt and matching jacket over a white blouse with ruffles down the front. Clay guessed she was fifteen or sixteen years old.

Behind them a buckboard driven too fast by Junior bounced into the ranch yard. Two large trunks in the wagon bed slid to the front as Junior loudly halted the team and set the brake.

'Clay,' Rawls said, ignoring the rattling buckboard and cloud of dust settling over them, 'get a couple of the hands and lug Annie's trunks to her room.' Then, like the father of the bride, Rawls took the girl by the arm and led her to the ranch house.

Junior leaped off the wagon seat and strutted after them, wearing a new hat and, for once, clean clothes. Trailing behind him was a strong odour of bay-rum hair tonic.

During most of the next two weeks Clay was away from the home ranch. He and Specs stocked the two line shacks with winter provisions and firewood, and worked with the cowhands to move the last of the Circle R stock onto winter range.

One day strangers were seen crossing the Circle R. Specs and two cowhands were drifting stock toward the south sector of the ranch when four men with pack animals rode over the crest of a grassy hill a quarter of a mile away. Specs hailed them, but the men pulled back and quickly rode out of sight.

Upon learning this, Clay ordered four of his men to patrol Circle R range for the next several days. Clay himself rode across the rolling grasslands from one waterhole to the next, searching for the blackened signs of recent campfires and fresh tracks.

He found nothing, and neither did the cowhands on patrol. The strangers might have been hunters who simply didn't want to explain why they were there. Or they could have been criminals fleeing Canada, entering the country on the old Blackfoot Indian trail over Squaw Peak.

'Gold prospectors, maybe,' Specs suggested, 'who got run out of the mountains by a storm.'

Clay thought this was possible, but unlikely this late in the year. He doubted the men were rustlers, either, but wished he'd had a chance to look at the brands on the strangers' pack animals.

After dark on payday Clay returned to the home ranch and went into his cabin. He learned from Cookie that Junior had been stumbling over himself to court Annie. So far, Cookie observed, he wasn't getting the time of day from her.

'You oughta see that young buck parading around here in stiff new clothes like he'd just stepped out of a Remington painting,' Cookie said, chuckling. 'Hell, he can't hardly sit a horse that ain't been gentled down for a sidesaddle.'

'What does the Old Man think about this

courtship?' Clay asked.

'When it comes to that kid,' Cookie said, shaking his head, 'Rawls don't see anything he don't want to see.'

The next morning Junior failed to show up for breakfast, and Clay couldn't find him in either the horse barn or the bunkhouse. But after a more careful search, Clay saw that his belongings were gone. The black quarter-horse mare Junior rode was missing, along with a bridle and saddle.

'I dunno, I dunno,' Rawls said dully when Clay went into the main room of the ranch house and reported the missing Circle R horse and gear. The Old Man slouched in his favorite chair made of elk antlers bound together by tightened strips of rawhide.

Clay said, 'Yesterday was payday.'

Rawls interpreted the remark differently from the way Clay meant it. 'Maybe Junior rode to town to buy some new duds,' the Old Man said with a glimmer of hope in his voice. 'He's been cleaning himself up lately. Have you noticed that, Clay?'

Out of the corner of his eye Clay saw Annie slowly move into the open doorway of her room. When he looked at her, she bowed her head and ventured in.

'I don't know where Junior went,' Annie said in a soft voice, 'but I know why he left the ranch.'

Rawls turned to her in surprise.

Annie looked up, meeting the Old Man's gaze. 'I never once encouraged his attentions, Jess, but I had to stop him. I had to tell him–'

Her voice broke and she cupped her face in her hands. 'I have to tell you why ... why Mother and Grandma sent me out here. I'm ... I'm going to have a baby.'

Clay hitched Rawls's horse to the buggy and drove the Old Man to Yellow Pine. The air was cold and still, but in the sky over the northern horizon thick, gray clouds boiled.

'That damned sister of mine,' Rawls growled, 'keeping a secret like that from me. Probably figured I wouldn't take Annie in if I knowed the truth right off.' Sheepskin coat wrapped around him, collar upturned, and his battered Stetson pulled low on his head, Rawls sat in silence for a mile. Then he muttered, 'Well, she's gonna get a letter from me that'll smoke from here to Baltimore.'

Clay drove the buggy down Yellow Pine's rutted street, stopping at the hitching rail in front of Mays's General Store & Post Office. The building was frame, made to appear larger by a tall false front. Inside the store, bins and crates and glass display cases contained everything needed by cowhands, ranchers, and their wives and children. The store supplied everything from horseshoe nails to stick candy, from whalebone corsets to plug tobacco.

Al Mays was a tall, angular man with a long beard and dark hair combed straight back from his forehead. Wiping his hands on his apron, Mays moved behind a big counter that held his cash register.

'Howdy!' he greeted Clay and the Old Man loudly.

Rawls moved to the counter and asked, 'That wrangler of mine stop in here yesterday evening?'

The storekeeper nodded and grinned. 'Just before dark he stopped in and bought a gunnysack full of grub.' His smile faded and he added uneasily, 'The kid charged the grub to the Circle R, just like he did the duds he's bought lately.'

Rawls pursed his lips.

'Something wrong, Jess?' Mays asked.

'Nope,' Rawls said.

Clay looked at a row of pigeon holes on one wall that served as the post office. The Circle R mail slot was empty. Wanted posters were tacked on the wall there, and Clay scanned them. As ranch foreman, he suspected he'd hired some of these men over the years, but he had a policy of never questioning the name a man gave, or asking about his back trail. Clay hired on instinct mostly, never faulting a cowhand as long as the work got done.

Rawls asked, 'Where'd the kid go when he

left here?'

Mays thought a moment, then gestured over his shoulder to a glassed liquor cabinet. 'Besides the grub, he charged a bottle of bourbon. Then he headed down to Dirty Gertie's. I'm thinking, now there goes a pup who's looking to grow up quick.'

Rawls turned and strode to the front door.

'Al,' Clay asked, 'you hear any talk about cattle rustlers hitting the ranches around here – the Lazy T, the DHS, or any of the smaller outfits?'

Mays shook his head. 'I heard about your trouble, but not any other ranches, Clay. A rumor's floating around that the Stock-growers Association is hiring range detectives to patrol the grasslands this spring.'

'About damned time we got something for the dues we pay in to that outfit,' Rawls said over his shoulder as he pulled the door open.

Clay followed the Old Man into the cold outside, and climbed into the buggy after him.

'Let's go talk to that woman,' Rawls said.

Clay took up the reins and turned the horse. As the buggy swung around, he saw that the warehouse foundation at the far end of the railroad platform was completed, and the railroad cars housing the Majestic crew were gone.

Clay urged the horse across Cottonwood

Creek, and reined to a halt in front of the low cabin. As he climbed out of the buggy, the plank door opened and a huge woman emerged from the darkness within.

'Howdy, boys,' Gertie said.

Rawls got out of the buggy and strode to her. 'Is my wrangler still here?'

Clay moved beside the Old Man and looked at Gertie's fat face, white as flour. Her eyes, dark and tiny, were nearly buried by mounds of flesh that bulged up from her cheeks. She wore a threadbare gown, probably the same one Clay had last seen her wearing, and on her feet were beaded buckskin moccasins, surprisingly small in size.

'The kid's gone,' she said.

'Where?' Rawls demanded.

Gertie blinked, then slowly shook her head. 'He never said.'

Rawls reached into his trouser pocket and pulled out a five-dollar gold piece. Moving a step closer to the woman, he held the coin up to her face. 'You sure he didn't say where he was headed? Maybe he told you after he'd been drinking some?'

Gertie made no reply, but stared as though transfixed by the yellow coin under her eyes.

Clay was uncertain whether the woman was drunk or dim-witted, or both. On occasion he'd come here searching for a missing cowhand, and Gertie was always like this, as big and slow as an enormous ewe.

Now she smiled faintly, holding out a puffed hand, somehow imagining that by doing so she would possess that money.

To Clay's amazement, Rawls shoved the gold coin into her hand. 'If that kid comes back,' Rawls said, 'get word to me, hear?'

Gertie nodded, her smile broadening enough to show missing teeth. 'I'll do that, Mr Rawls.' She drew her clenched hand deep into her breasts, as though afraid he would change his mind and snatch the coin away from her.

On the way back to the home ranch, Clay asked, 'Why are you working so hard to pick up Junior's trail, Jess? Did he steal something I don't know about?'

Rawls cast a critical glance at his foreman. 'I know what you think of the kid, Clay, but I've got a different angle on him. When I look at Junior, I see something of myself.'

'That's hard to figure,' Clay said.

'Might sound loco to you,' Rawls said, 'but you didn't know me half a century ago. I was as worthless as tits on a boar, and I had a big mad brewing inside me. Wanted to fight all the time. Oh, I was plumb dangerous when I was sixteen, seventeen years old.'

Rawls paused, looking at Clay. 'Now ain't that how you've got the kid figured?'

Clay nodded.

'Well, I changed,' Rawls said, 'after I went

to work for a man who owned a big dairy farm. That was back in Maryland, a lifetime or two ago. He worked me from dawn to dark, until I thought I'd drop.

'Hell, I can't put into words how it happened. This man I worked for and got to know was a feller who put ever'thing he had, ever' minute of his life, into that dairy farm. But to him that place was more than a farm, see? Well, I got the idea that I wanted the same feeling out of life.

'I wore a blue uniform 'til 1865, and then I wandered some, but I never lost that idea. When I heard about ranching in this wild country, I somehow knowed that's what I was hunting. I knowed I'd found my life's work.'

Clay listened to the steady *clip-clop* of the horse's hooves as the Old Man fell silent for a time.

'Well,' Rawls went on, 'I figured if I could shove that same notion into Junior's young head, I'd be passing along something important, that's all.'

'I admire you for that, Jess,' Clay said. But he was mystified. If what the kid needed was a dose of good, hard work, why didn't Jess stand over him and work him from dawn to dark? And why did he let Junior get away with bothering Annie?

Clay recalled Cookie's remark, *When it comes to that kid, Rawls don't see anything he don't want to see.*

True enough, Clay thought. Rawls had a blind spot there. Yet Clay felt moved by the Old Man's motives. Rawls meant well, and he was right in believing that young men do change in time. Clay began to wonder if he'd been too hard on Junior.

But as they drove into the long, fertile valley that embraced the home ranch, he reflected that Junior was not just a smart-mouthed kid with no purpose in life. Junior had shown a streak of meanness. And he was a thief.

CHAPTER 8

Clay left the home ranch at noon and rode south to make a circuit of the line shacks. Snows would come at any time now, and he wanted to make sure the cowhands were in place and their provisions complete.

He followed a meandering creek bottom that wound through the low, grassy hills of the ranch's south sector. In the cold, stiffened mud along the bank he saw the imprinted tracks of birds, rabbits, and deer.

Ten or twelve miles away from the home ranch Clay came upon fresh tracks of a shod horse. He reined up where the tracks crossed the creek. The hoof prints were unusually small, and as Clay studied them, his horse nickered and tossed his head.

Clay looked up. On the crest of the hill across the creek emerged a dark, rounded shape. Before Clay could react to the sight of a man's hat, he saw a puff of smoke.

The sound of the shot came an instant before he was punched out of the saddle. Landing in the mud flat on his back, Clay felt the air rush out of his lungs. Dazed, he slowly realized that the warmth spreading over his chest was blood.

His eyes closed. He felt heavy and numb. Knowing he would sleep now, the thought passed through his mind that he would not awaken.

The day passed, and in darkness cold and still as a tomb Clay looked up into the starry sky. Far in the distance he heard a coyote yelp, and soon another answered with a long, lonely howl.

Clay turned his head from side to side. He became aware of a dull pain high in his chest. After a long moment, he raised a hand to the wound.

Blood was caked dry on his shirt and vest, and an inch or two below his collar bone was a moist hole. *I've been shot.* The realization still amazed him. He slowly rose on an elbow, seeing his horse by starlight. Asleep on its feet, the gelding stood beside the stream

65

twenty yards away.

Clay tried to sit, but fell back, moaning. He stared up at the night sky for a time, then slept again.

At sunrise Clay looked into an orange sky overhead. He was desperately thirsty. Grimacing against the pain that burst through his shoulder and upper chest, he rolled over into the shallow stream.

Cold water flowing past his face and down the length of his body revived him, and he drank in long gulps. Turning over on his back again left him drained of energy, and he fell into a deep sleep.

A steady tugging at his boot awakened him later in the morning. He opened his eyes and raised his head to see a young timber wolf biting his booted foot. It was tugging backward with quick, powerful jerks, as though tearing at a carcass.

Clay tried to shout, but no sound came. The wolf, yellow-eyed and muscular, intently gnawed at the cowhide boot, planting his front paws into the mud as he pulled. Clay felt his boot slip. The wolf growled, clamped down with powerful jaws, and pulled harder.

Reaching to his waist, Clay touched the walnut grips of his Colt .45. The fear of being eaten alive brought him alert, and suddenly he was thankful that his revolver had not fallen out of his holster.

Clay drew the gun and managed to cock

it. But he was too exhausted to hold his head up any longer. He lay back, aimed by memory, and pulled the trigger.

The Colt's roar came to his ears like a distant explosion. After a moment Clay raised his head again. The timber wolf lay at his feet, the top of its head blown away, one yellow gleaming eye dangling from the skull.

The horse was gone, run off by the wolf, probably. Now that Clay's mind had cleared, he knew he would never make it back to the home ranch. The line shack was even farther away. His only chance was to be found.

Clay raised the revolver into the air, thumbed back the hammer, and squeezed the trigger. He fired the gun two more times, rested, and then reloaded from his cartridge belt.

The sun was past its zenith when Clay fired his revolver three more times. As he lowered his arm, the gun fell from his hand. Losing strength, Clay knew he would not be able to fire his gun again. He closed his eyes.

Presently he became aware of a sound, a faint drumming that he felt through the ground more than he heard. He tried to concentrate, and slowly realized that a running horse was near, and coming closer.

'Over here, Jess!' Specs shouted. 'He's over here!'

Lying on his bunk, which had been moved

into the main room of the ranch house, Clay vaguely remembered being hefted onto the flatbed wagon driven by the Old Man. The ride back to the ranch house was a rough one, and he remembered hearing Rawls cuss and shout the same questions over his shoulder: 'Who did this to you, Clay? Who the hell shot you?'

Later Clay learned that his gelding had run back to the horse barn, and Specs and the Old Man had immediately started their search, thinking Clay had been thrown. The gunshots had led them to him.

Clay knew that if the timber wolf had been full-grown and hungry, the animal would have torn a leg off or gone for his throat. Even so, the young wolf had managed to chew through Clay's boot, and the thought of a bare foot for the critter to work on was not pleasant to consider.

Clay raised a hand to the bandage on his chest. His clothes had been cut off his body, he vaguely remembered, and he'd been doctored by Cookie.

'The bullet went clean through you, Clay,' Cookie said after cleaning the wound and tying the bandage tightly around his chest. 'I don't know how much blood you lost, but you ain't bleeding much now. That's a good sign, I reckon.'

For the next five days Clay slept more than he was awake. From time to time he was aware that Rawls, Cookie, and Specs stood over him, silently watching. As in a vivid dream, Clay thought he had died and was looking at his friends from his deathbed. He desperately wanted to break through and speak to these men who were his friends, but couldn't.

Clay was aware of Annie's presence, too. She changed his bandage every day, and the sweet, soft sound of her humming voice came to him. She spooned hot beef broth into his mouth, and when he grew stronger she brought oatmeal and coffee to him. On the ninth day he was able to sit up in bed.

'After you were found,' Annie told him, 'Jess gathered up all the men and sent them out to hunt down the ambusher. They didn't find anyone, but one herd of cattle had been scattered out of a pasture. Jess thinks you got too close to some rustlers, and after one of them shot you they ran off.'

Clay smiled faintly. 'From now on I'll ride the high ground.'

In the following days Clay was able to get out of bed and hobble around the ranch house. But he had little strength, and didn't go outside. He passed the time by ordering a new pair of boots out of the J.C. Hyer catalogue, and then he sat at a window, watching the first big storm of the year howl out of the north.

Snow piled up outside, and the wind carved

the white ocean into smoothly sculpted piles higher than a man on horseback. Rawls made Annie laugh when he came in from the barn and told her that a milk cow gave icicles in this weather.

Clay watched Annie sweep floors that had never been so clean, and help Cookie in the kitchen. In the evenings he listened as she read aloud from her leather-bound volumes of Robert Louis Stevenson and the American humorists Bill Nye and Mark Twain.

'Clay,' Rawls asked one evening, 'how'd we ever get along without Annie?'

From his bed Clay raised himself on an elbow and looked at the pair sitting in front of the fire. They faced one another. Rawls was slouched in his favorite chair, smoking his pipe, and Annie sat in a Queen Anne-style rocker Rawls had ordered for her from the Montgomery Ward catalogue.

'Poorly,' Clay replied.

Rawls took the pipe out of his mouth, and laughed heartily.

Clay exchanged a long look with Annie, and she smiled.

In the following house-bound days Clay talked with Annie, and as he got to know her better he found her to be more woman than girl. She was a hard worker who expressed no self-pity, and Clay never heard her complain about the Spartan conditions on the ranch.

In fact, she took to ranch life. She was no longer the shy, kittenlike girl Clay had seen step out of Rawls's buggy last month. She walked with a purposeful stride now, wearing work dresses of calico, and wearing her light brown hair in a braid that she wound in a circle pinned at the back of her head. In the evenings she combed her hair out so that it framed her face and shone in the firelight.

One morning after the Old Man had gone out to the barn to help Specs tend the animals, Annie brought a mug of coffee to Clay.

'I meant what I said the other night,' Clay told her.

'Since you've been here the Old Man has looked healthier, and he's in the best humor I've ever seen.'

She smiled. 'We talk a lot. I guess he needed someone who's a good listener.'

'It's more than that,' Clay said. 'You're family. Jess tried to adopt Junior and make him into family, but that didn't work. Now he's got you.'

Annie came and sat on the edge of the bed. 'Jess thinks a lot of you, Clay. The day he and Specs brought you in, he was afraid you were dying. We all were. You looked white as a bedsheet. Jess told me that he couldn't run the Circle R and ship beef without you.'

Clay shook his head slightly, seeing much irony in the fact that Rawls had said that to her, but never to him.

'Yesterday Jess told me that you're not a man who will be happy ramrodding another man's ranch forever,' Annie said. 'I think he worries about the future. About what will happen to this ranch.'

'The Old Man tells you a lot of things he's never said to me,' Clay said with a lopsided grin.

Annie shrugged. 'All you men ever talk about is cattle and weather and practical jokes.'

Clay laughed. 'I guess you're right about that.'

'What's in your future, Clay?' she asked suddenly. 'Will you stay here on the Circle R?'

He looked at her in surprise.

Annie's face reddened. 'Oh, I was too bold–'

Clay smiled at her. 'To tell you the truth, I hadn't thought much about the future until lately. I've had plenty of time to let my mind wander. Laying out there in the mud with a hole in my chest, I wasn't too clearheaded. But I remember thinking that I didn't have much to show for my life. I own a couple of horses, a change of clothes, a few dollars in Frenchy's safe, and that's about it.'

He paused. 'While I've been laid up here,

72

I've daydreamed about a ranch with my name on the deed. And a family someday.' Looking at her, he said, 'Tell me about your future, Annie.'

'The past seems more important than the future,' she said.

'You're too young to talk that way,' Clay said.

Eyes downcast, she shook her head. Her lower lip quivered.

'Well, it's none of my business,' Clay said.

She raised her head abruptly and looked into his eyes. Suddenly a torrent of words and tears came out of her.

'He's dead now, the minister of my family's church... Shot himself, found out I was pregnant by him... After I have the baby, I'm supposed to give it up for adoption, go back to school...' She sobbed into her hands. 'I'll never ... never give up my baby.'

Clay reached out and laid his hand on her quaking shoulder. 'I'm sorry, Annie.'

She wiped her hands against her dress in a childlike motion, but a moment later she took a deep breath and regained her womanly composure.

'I shouldn't unload my problems on you Clay,' she said, standing.

He watched her turn and walk into the kitchen.

CHAPTER 9

In six weeks Clay's wound had healed to a reddened scar the size of a half dollar. He'd regained much of his strength, and was feeling increasingly grouchy with a severe case of cabin fever.

Over the protests of Annie and the Old Man, Clay pronounced himself recovered, and went to work with Specs. Specs had handled the chores up to now, but Clay knew the work was too much for one man all winter, and too dangerous.

Together they hauled hay on sleds to the far-flung herds of cattle, and every week they axed open waterholes that had frozen over with several inches of ice. The land was clenched in the cold grip of winter, a season that always seemed endless to Clay, and keeping animals alive now was relentless, risky work. A man could loose his bearings in wind-driven snow and wander to his death.

For this reason Clay insisted the men work in pairs, and if a storm appeared to be brewing, he sent the cowhands back to the line shacks or the home ranch. When a storm passed, they would return to the range again, their saddle horses bucking snowdrifts.

Because the men kept close track of the stock and prevented storm-scattered herds from piling against the drift fence, the Circle R came through the winter of 1894–95 with few losses.

The icy grip of that season was abruptly broken when a gust of warm air swept across the snow-covered grasslands. This Chinook wind announced spring's arrival, and within a few days patches of brown grass bent flat to the earth showed through the white landscape.

Clay saw little of Annie after he moved his bunk into his cabin and returned to work. Sometimes he would talk with her while he ate a quick breakfast at sunrise, or in the evening when he came into the ranch house to report to the Old Man.

At these times Annie wore a heavy robe as she curled in her rocking chair by the fire. Clay would come in with a cup of coffee laced with condensed milk and whiskey, kneel by the dancing flames in the fire place, and talk to Rawls and to Annie.

Clay was amazed one warm spring morning when he looked out the front door of his cabin and saw her waddling across the yard from the pump to the ranch house. Instead of her robe, she wore a long skirt with a white blouse, untucked.

Last winter she had started to show, but

now – suddenly, it seemed to Clay – she blossomed with child. Her frame seemed too small, her shoulders too narrow, for the growing burden she carried.

Clay left his cabin and rushed to her side. He grasped her arm above the elbow and helped her to the ranch house. Annie smiled tiredly at him. On the porch of the house stood Rawls, hands on his hips, grinning.

'Spring calving time,' he said with a wink.

'I'll take her to the Lazy T,' Clay said. To Annie he explained, 'A woman is there.'

Rawls said, 'Good idea.'

'I'm not that close to my time,' Annie protested. 'You men panic too easily.'

Rawls chuckled as Clay helped her up the three porch steps, touching her gently as though handling loose eggs.

For the next several days Clay stayed near the ranch house. He worked with Specs at clean-up chores, digging a trash hole and then shoveling into it a winter's collection of rusty cans, bottles, and bones, all exposed by melting snows.

Clay filled out his spring crew from the cowhands who drifted into the home ranch. Some of the men were new to Clay, but many had worked either on the Circle R or nearby ranches for the last several years.

Among the trail weary cowhands who came looking for work were Curly and Wash. Clay was shoveling stove and fireplace ashes into the outhouse vaults behind the bunkhouse when he saw the two men coming from the direction of Yellow Pine. Recognizing the pair by the way they sat in their saddles, Clay put his shovel down and walked out into the yard.

'We heard about the Bear Paw gold boom all the way down to the Mexican border,' Curly said, reining up his horse. Wash stopped beside him. Neither man dismounted without an invitation.

'Yellow Pine doesn't look like the same place,' Wash said. 'You'll have your hands full this year, Clay.'

'Yeah, we figured you'd need a couple of top hands,' Curly said.

Clay nodded. 'That I do. You know where I can find any?'

Curly and Wash exchanged glances. 'Ungrateful son, ain't he?' Wash said.

'Damn sure is,' Curly replied. 'And to think of all the trouble we went to protecting the good name of Clay Scarborough all winter.'

'How'd you do that?' Clay asked.

'Wasn't easy,' Wash said.

'No, it wasn't,' Curly explained. 'Ever' time we told the true story of how you pulled your gun on a real jackass, folks just laughed.'

'But we swore up and down that the donkey shot first,' Wash said.

'That's right,' Curly said. 'We told folks

that's how Clay Scarborough of the Circle R saved our lives.'

'Well, I do appreciate that,' Clay said.

'Glad to hear it,' Curly said. 'For a minute there I thought we'd blistered our butts riding up here just to get insulted.'

Clay grinned and said, 'Truth is, I'm a little surprised to see you after what happened last year.'

Wash said, 'We're here to work for you, Clay.'

'We both know who keeps this ranch going,' Curly added.

'That gets harder every year, doesn't it?' Wash asked.

'Seems like it,' Clay said. 'The Old Man's in a better humor nowadays, though.'

'That stinking kid still here?' Curly asked.

Clay shook his head. 'Junior rode out after a payday last winter. It's a long story. I'll tell it to you one of these days.' He motioned toward the barn. 'Turn your horses into the corral and get yourselves a couple of bunks.'

Watching the two men rein their horses around, leading their spare mounts, Clay mentally reviewed his crew. He'd hired more men this year than had ever worked on the Circle R, which meant more cowhands to supervise and probably meant more problems for him. But a larger crew also meant a show of force. Rustlers would think twice before hitting a Circle R herd. At least

Clay hoped so.

Warm weather greened hay meadows, and the air became scented by blooming wild roses. Snow water filled the lowlands, and from these sky-reflecting pools rivulets trickled into tributaries of Cottonwood Creek.

That stream swelled high in banks lined with tall, leafy willows. And with the sounds of rushing water came the sounds of life as birds sang to warm mornings and insects swarmed out of the damp earth. In the pastures calves ventured farther and farther away from their mothers, and colts and fillies leaped in rollicking play.

The first big job of the season on the Circle R was to round up the horses. Young ones, now weaned, had to be roped and branded. The males would be gelded, then saddle- and halter-broken. For the job of bronc-busting, Clay hired Roy Long Knife.

A swarthy, silent man of unknown background, Roy Long Knife lived on the Blackfoot Indian reservation for much of the year, but every spring he showed up on the Circle R as he moved through the Montana ranch country.

He slept in the loft of the horse barn and took his meals outside the kitchen door. Neither Indian nor white, he was disliked by the cowhands who instinctively distrusted a man armed with a long-bladed knife on his belt instead of a revolver. But no one doubted the man's ability to handle horses, from gentling the young ones to the neck-snapping, bone-crushing work of breaking wild broncs.

Among the horses herded into the fenced pasture below the barn were several outlaws that had never been saddle-broken, even by Roy Long Knife. These were fine animals in appearance, sleek and strong, whose wills remained unbroken. Tired of bucking and rearing, they'd sooner bite a man or lie flat on the ground than wear a saddle and bridle.

What to do with these outlaws was a long-standing controversy between Clay and the Old Man. The geldings were not truly wild, so they stayed on the Circle R range, eating Circle R grass. Their favorite meadows became overgrazed. And then when the snows came, they raided hay put out for cattle.

Clay wanted to sell the horses to a slaughterhouse or shoot them, but Old Man couldn't bring himself to do either. So they were allowed to run and eat, and every spring after horse roundup when Clay brought up the subject of the outlaw geldings, a distant look came into Rawls's eyes.

'I know you're right, Clay,' he'd say, 'but they're so damned purty.'

In late afternoon Clay rode in with the last

bunch of horses that the cowhands had gathered, and he helped haze them into the fenced pasture with the main herd.

Inside a pole corral near the barn, Roy Long Knife was at work. Roy wore a red bandanna tied around his head, Indian style, but on his feet were boots with three-inch heels.

A rangy bronc, brown with a blaze face, was bucking hard and whirling, doing his best to throw the man who clung to his back. Clay watched as the horse bucked himself out, and soon Roy Long Knife was guiding him around the corral, gently rubbing the animal's twitching neck. Now 'green-broke,' the horse would be turned over to one of the cowhands who would complete the job of training him for a useful cow pony.

Clay liked this season. Spring meant a new start on the ranch, even though the work was much the same every year. Something about the fresh smell in the air, the half-wild horses milling in the corrals, and the anticipation of all the jobs that lay ahead filled Clay with a sense of eagerness. More than hard work, the season meant a celebration of winter's broken grip. Now everyone, even the critters, were bursting with exuberant energy.

Even the Old Man was caught up in it. For the past several days he had come out of the ranch house to join the 'rail birds,' those cowhands who sat on the top pole of the corral to watch Roy Long Knife earn his ten dollars per head.

Rawls wasn't here this afternoon, and Clay moved around the corral to a spot where he could look past the log barn to the ranch house. What he saw there brought a sudden, wintry change of mood.

A black mare with a Circle R brand was tied to the post in front of the house. Clay knew immediately that Junior had returned.

CHAPTER 10

Clay entered the ranch house through the kitchen. Cookie was there, wearing his white apron and bent over a mound of bread dough that he was kneading.

'Romeo's back,' Cookie said over his shoulder.

'So I see,' Clay said. He moved past Cookie and went into the main room of the house. Junior sat in the Old Man's favorite chair, and Rawls stood nearby, grinning.

'Clay,' Rawls said, 'I was about to hunt for you. We need to have a little talk.'

'That we do,' Clay said, stopping a few paces away from them. He noticed that the door to Annie's room was closed.

Junior stood and came toward Clay, holding out his hand to shake. 'I owe you an apology.'

For a moment Clay stared at the kid's outstretched hand. Junior was dressed in clothes Clay recognized from the shelves of Al Mays's General Store, much worn now. The big Remington army revolver hung at his right hip, the bottom of the holster tied around his thigh.

'Last year I was a pain in the ass around here,' Junior said, 'and 'I'm sorry.'

While the Old Man looked on expectantly, Clay reached out and briefly shook Junior's hand.

'Well, now,' Rawls said happily, 'we can get on with our business. Clay I've hired Junior to ride for us. I want him to help out with the roundup. Get somebody else to do the wrangling chores. Out on the range you can show Junior the ropes–'

'Jess,' Clay interrupted, 'during spring roundup I don't have time to teach anybody anything.'

'Well, I know, Clay,' Rawls said, 'but Junior can watch, and you can give him a few pointers as you go.'

'I'm ready to work as a cowhand,' Junior said. 'I spent all winter on a ranch down in Wyoming, and I learned a lot about riding and roping, things you never had time to teach me up here.'

Clay looked at the kid steadily. 'You were taught as much as you wanted to learn.'

'Now, now,' Rawls said, moving a step closer, 'I won't have you two arguing.'

'Look, Clay,' Junior said, 'I know you've got your doubts about me. I don't blame you. I caused trouble for you, and like I said, I'm sorry. All I'm asking how is a second chance. I'll work hard, and I'll get along with the crew.' He added, 'If I don't prove myself, I'll leave.'

'There, now, Clay,' Rawls said, 'what more can you ask of the young man.'

'One more thing,' Clay said to Junior. 'You work for me around here. You do what I tell you, and don't come in here complaining to Jess. Understood?'

'Sure,' Junior said, 'I understand. You're the ramrod.' He cast a smile at Rawls, then said, 'You won't regret this, Clay. I'm a hard worker. You'll see.'

Clay exhaled, seeing the happy expression on Rawls's face. Evidently he had forgiven Junior's theft of the mare and gear, and running up a bill at Mays's General Store.

Clay saw he had little choice in this matter. He would either hire the kid or be overruled by the Old Man. At least he had straightened out his relationship with Junior. He hoped Rawls would make it stick when the going got tough.

Saturday night in Frenchy's Bon Ton Saloon, Clay stood at the bar, a hand-rolled Bull Durham cigarette dangling from the fingers of one hand and a mug half full of beer in the other. He absently listened to the hum of men's voices and occasional drunken singing, followed by rough laughter.

'Never was a bronc never got rode,
Never was a rider never got thronged.'

Riding into town that evening, Clay had seen for himself what the cowhands had been telling him. Yellow Pine had mushroomed into a tent town, and the big warehouse by the railroad tracks was nearly completed.

Dozens of white canvas tents, connected by a network of boardwalks, housed construction workers, carpenters, and prospectors on their way to the gold district. In other tents, many with plank sides, were barber shops and bath houses, a variety of stores, saloons, and gambling dens.

Beyond these structures on the grassy flat above Cottonwood Creek was a row of cribs for the women who followed the men to the boom town. This section of hastily built shacks and small tents was already locally known as 'Four-bit Flats.'

The Bon Ton was more crowded tonight than Clay had ever seen it, but he noticed that the saloon remained a watering hole for cowhands. Sprinkled among the men wearing Stetsons were a few railroad and construction workers, and seated at the gaming tables in the back of the room were several professional gamblers. They were well-dressed, sober men with string ties on white shirts, and clean hats.

Clay turned and leaned back on his elbows against the bar. Through the pale, smoky light cast by lanterns, he saw familiar faces under the curled brims of Stetsons. His own crew was here, along with cowhands from surrounding ranches. Earlier, Junior had appeared at the front door of the saloon, but quickly turned away when Frenchy saw him. The kid has yet to make his peace here, Clay thought.

Seated at one of the gaming tables was Curly, hat pushed back on his head as he studied the five cards in his hand. Other Circle R men Clay saw in the crowed were Zeb Hayes, Mike Walters, John Leed, Jack Grayson, and Hank Brown.

Wash stood at the bar beside Clay, and next to him was a lean cowhand who had worked on the Circle R for the last three seasons, Bill Clark. Bill was a talker, one of the bunkhouse orators.

All the cowhands were in a mood to celebrate, knowing they would not return for two weeks or so. Now that the horses had been rounded up, branded, doctored, and green-broke, spring cattle roundup would begin throughout northern Montana. Besides drinking and shooting-the-bull in the Bon Ton, the cowhands would tour tent town, and many would end up in Four-bit Flats sometime before daylight.

'Hey, Frenchy.'

Clay turned to the bar when Bill Clark called to the saloonkeeper.

'Whatever happened to that Frenchman on trial over there in Paris, that Dreyfus fella?' Bill asked. He was a long-faced man with a hawklike nose and high cheekbones.

Frenchy drew a beer from a tapped barrel before answering. 'Alfred Dreyfus was convicted. He is in prison now.'

'I'll be damned,' Bill said matter-of-factly. 'So he was guilty of selling military secrets to the Germans, was he?'

Frenchy slid the mug of foaming beer down the bar, then turned and leaned close to the cowhand. 'No, my friend, Alfred Dreyfus is guilty of being a Jew.'

'What the hell does that have to do with it?' Bill asked. 'He was an officer in the French artillery corps. I never read nothing about him being a Jew.'

'It is so,' Frenchy said. He added, 'For the same reason, I left my country.'

Clay listened to this single clue to Frenchy's past, the first he'd heard from the man.

'Because you're a Jew?' Bill asked, his forehead winking as he considered this. 'I don't get it.'

'I am happy for that,' Frenchy said. 'I hope that poison never takes over America.' He moved down the bar where he drew another mug. After setting it up, he scooped coins off the edge of the bar, came back, and dropped them in the coin box.

'In my country, you see, some important men in the military and in the government want to bring back the monarchy, the king. They seek ways to start a revolution. These powerful men blame the Jews for France's troubles, and Alfred Dreyfus was one of their victims.'

Suddenly there was a disturbance at the back of the saloon. Clay saw men scurrying and backing away from a poker game at one of the gambling tables. Frenchy quickly ducked down behind the bar, and came up with a sawed-off double-barreled shotgun.

Clay looked past Wash, half expecting to see Curly start a brawl. Wash must have had the same thought, for he pushed through the crowd to make his way back there.

But Curly was not involved. In the back of the saloon Clay saw two men facing each other over a table, deadly silent. One was a gambler dressed in a broadcloth suit with red buttons down the front. The other man Clay recognized as a cowhand from the

DHS Ranch.

The cowhand was crimson-faced from too much whiskey or anger, or both. He had risen from his chair in a crouch. His left hand gripped the butt of his holstered revolver, reminding Clay of the man's nickname: Lefty.

Across the round table the gambler eyed his adversary, keeping his hands palm down on the table top. His small dark eyes and thin nose gave him the appearance of a lizard. This impression was heightened by his dark sideburns which were sharply angled toward a mustache as thin as wire.

'You've had enough,' the gambler said, his voice carrying across the silent saloon. 'Go home.'

'Cleaned me out, you bastard,' Lefty said.

'Sometimes lady luck is at your side,' the gambler replied, 'sometimes she's at mine.'

'Luck, hell,' Lefty said. He nodded at the stacks of gold and silver coins on the table in front of the gambler. 'You win too much for luck.'

'You can prove my dishonesty?' the gambler asked.

'I'm not the only man you've picked clean,' he said. 'That's proof enough.'

'I wager when I hold a winning hand,' the gambler said with a slight shrug. 'That's my trick of the trade.'

Disgusted, Lefty spat a shiny brown gob

that landed on the gambler's shirt front. Men in the saloon edged farther away, crowding each other against the log walls.

Clay saw the gambler smile.

Lefty yanked out his revolver, but at almost the same instant the gambler lifted his hand, revealing a derringer. He snatched it up, and the shot from it was barely louder than the snapping of a man's fingers.

Lefty cried out. His revolver fell to the dirt floor as he grasped his shoulder. Blood seeped through his fingers, and he sank to his knees.

The gambler stood and reloaded his derringer. 'Next time you see me, turn away – or I'll kill you.' He took off his low-crowned hat and turned it upside down. Bringing it to the edge of the table, he swept his winnings into it, then strode through the parting crowd to the door.

Friends rushed to Lefty's side. They bandaged his shoulder with handkerchiefs and stopped the bleeding. A few minutes later Lefty was helped to his feet and taken outside.

Card games at other tables soon broke up. The cowhands no longer laughed or sang. Instead they spoke in hushed voices, or drank silently.

Clay was joined at the bar by Curly and Wash, and the three of them talked late into the night. Clay told them about the winter before on the Circle R, and then he listened to their stories about herding Mexican cattle on an Arizona ranch.

At first light the next morning, before Clay's head cleared from a long, beery night in the Bon Ton, he was awakened by Cookie.

'It's Annie, Clay,' he said. 'She's having pains, real regular now. She's calling for you.'

CHAPTER 11

Clay yanked on his trousers and ran sock-footed across the yard to the ranch house. He rushed inside and strode through the darkened kitchen to the front room. Annie's bedroom door was open. A single lamp burned beside her bed.

Clay entered the room and stopped abruptly. Annie lay on top of the sheets, her face gleaming with sweat. The light flannel nightgown she wore clung to her swollen body.

'Clay,' she said hoarsely. 'Clay.'

He went to her bedside and grasped her outstretched hand in his. Her grip was strong.

'I'm going to have my baby,' she whispered.

'I'll hitch up the buggy and drive to the

Lazy T,' Clay said. 'I'll bring the rancher's wife.'

Annie shook her head. 'No time. I need you here.'

Clay looked at Cookie who stood in the doorway. The man's lined face was grim. 'Where's Rawls?'

'Asleep,' Cookie said. 'I didn't see no point in bringing him into this.'

Annie moaned as a labor pain surged through her.

'Looks like we're going to deliver a baby,' Clay said to the ranch cook. 'Go heat a tub of water and get a bunch of towels ready.'

Sunrise that day was greeted by the first cries of a baby boy. Rousted out of his bed, the Old Man was at first angry that he had not been awakened sooner. But when he hobbled sleepily into Annie's bedroom and saw the pink infant in her arms, his mood quickly changed. He grinned, proud as a grandfather.

'Ain't this something?' he said over and over again. 'Ain't this something?'

It had been something, all right, Clay thought. Over the years he'd lent a helping hand in the birth of many calves and colts and fillies, but he'd never experienced anything so profound – or so terrifying – as the birth of this infant boy.

Clay went back to his cabin after breakfast

and fell into his bunk, exhausted. He thought of all that could have gone wrong but didn't, and he felt a great admiration for Annie. She'd remained fearless throughout, clenching her jaw against the pain. After giving birth to a healthy, squalling boy, she'd bathed and nursed the infant.

Later in the day Annie received visitors. All the cowhands of the Circle R, hats in hand, marched past her bed in solemn procession. Outside the bedroom they argued over a suitable name for this ranch-born child.

The choice was announced by Annie, leaving the selection of a nickname to the cowhands. The boy would be known by his mother's last name, Davenport. His first name would be William, for his deceased father. William J. Davenport. The J stood for Jess.

After supper the next evening Clay saw Roy Long Knife leave the ranch house and go into the horse barn. Realizing the man had been paid for the season's bronc-busting and was leaving the Circle R, Clay followed him.

Deep in the shadows of the barn's stalls, Clay, moving soundlessly down the runway, looked for him. He found Roy in a stall near the far end of the barn, throwing his saddle on his spotted horse.

'Roy.'

Whirling, Roy Long Knife thrust his hand to the sheathed knife on his hip.

Clay raised his hands. 'I'm peaceful.'

A brief smile crossed the man's swarthy face. 'Don't ever sneak up on a man who's just been paid.'

'Didn't aim to sneak up,' Clay said. 'I wanted to catch you before you rode out so we could talk about a job.'

'Breaking horses?' Roy asked, turning to his Indian pony and knotting the cinch. 'I'm due at the DHS in a couple days.'

'I had something else in mind,' Clay said. 'I'm looking for an outrider.'

'Outrider?' Roy said, looking at Clay. The man's heavy features – blunt chin, broad nose, and large dark eyes – showed little emotion, and many men did not trust him. But over the past few years Clay had sensed that Roy was an intelligent, perceptive man, more so than he let on, and was loyal to those he respected.

'I need a man who knows the country,' Clay said, 'and doesn't mind keeping to himself.'

Roy pulled the cinch tight and took down the stirrup, then rested his arms on the saddle. 'Expecting trouble?'

'I want to be ready, that's all,' Clay said. 'I need a good man who'll be my eyes and ears. You know this country better than any man around here. If you'll ride Circle R

94

range and report privately to me, I'll see that you're well paid.'

Roy studied him. 'Report to you, and not to the Old Man?'

Clay nodded. 'I report to the Old Man.'

Roy thought for several moments, then said, 'I'll ride for you, Clay.'

'Good,' Clay said. 'Start work when you finish busting horses at the DHS.'

'All right,' Roy said. He paused and asked, 'You think some of your crew might be throwing a wide loop?'

'I doubt it,' Clay said. 'But I've got a big crew this year. Some of these men are new to me.'

Before Roy Long Knife rode out, Clay loaned him his 30.06 Winchester along with a saddle boot to go with it. This was an act of faith and proved that Clay trusted him.

In the morning Clay met the cowhands at the horse corral. He divided them into four groups. In each was at least one man who knew Circle R range. Clay described the areas they would be responsible for, making certain the knowledgeable cowhand in each group was aware of which rock outcroppings, which gullies, which coulees he was talking about.

Their job was to systematically scour the vast south sector of the ranch for strays. Along with the scattered herds, the cowhands would find steers that had wintered in small bunches, and by now were as wild and wily as mule deer.

In making assignments, Clay took into consideration the men who worked well together, and he kept intact partners like Curly and Wash. When his gaze fell to Junior, Clay said, 'You'll ride with me today.'

Junior replied with a single nod of his head, imitating the curt gesture made by the seasoned cowhands as they received their assignments.

As in past years, the hub of the Circle R spring gather would be in a huge natural bowl located near the drift fence. In the circular lowland where there was both grass and water, the herds of cattle would be brought together and controlled by riders for a tally and the branding of calves.

Cookie drove the chuck wagon to the roundup campsite on a rise overlooking the bowl, and Specs followed with the bed wagon. Clay and Junior rode along with them on horseback. The air was warmed by the morning sun, and the angle of light turned the land pale green, a beautiful colour of new grass that was unique to this time of year.

An hour before noon they reached the campsite. Clay reined up, looking down at the roundup ground. On the edge was a branding corral, built a quarter of a century before by the Old Man. The weathered poles were cracked and split. Every year the poles were repaired with more nails and twists of wire, and every year Clay silently predicted the corral would not last another season. But Specs always managed to put the thing together again.

As Clay looked across the land and saw the fresh grass, the old corral, and a circle of blue that was a spring-fed pond, he thought that he would like to bring Annie here and show her this place.

Clay and Junior helped Cookie pitch the mess tent, and then assembled the sheet-iron camp stove inside. Specs had gone to work on the corral.

At noon the four of them sat in the shade of the wagons and ate beef sandwiches. Clay savored the peace and quiet. Soon the air would be dusty, filled with the shouts and whistles of cowhands, the bawling of milling cattle, and the smells of sweating men and animals.

'Time to get this thing going,' Clay said, getting to his feet after he finished eating. Junior followed him, and they mounted their horses and rode south and east, angling toward the drift fence.

Clay had noticed some changes in Junior, changes for the better. The kid was quieter this year, more guarded in his remarks. And he kept himself cleaner. He'd taken a bunk in the bunkhouse, and evidently did not want to be tossed into the horse trough this year.

But still the kid's face had a sullen cast and a blank stare that made Clay wonder: What the hell is going through his head now?

Clay knew that the men remembered what Junior was like last year. So he was watchful for tensions among the men, signs that problems might be brewing between the kid and the cowhands.

He noticed that Junior kept his distance from Curly and Wash, and seemed to be trying to avoid trouble. Junior spent little time in the ranch house with Rawls, perhaps in an effort to win acceptance by the cowhands. Either that, or Junior realized the Old Man was giving his full attention to Annie and the baby now and didn't want the competition.

When they reached the long wire fence, Clay turned east and followed it. With Junior flanking him, he rode on to one of the Circle R line shacks more than a mile away.

Used only in the winter, the shack was a log dugout cut into the side of a hill. It was surrounded by brush, and after a summer's growth on the hillside, a man had to know where to look to find it. But today the shack stood out clearly.

As Clay rode toward the line shack, he leaned over in the saddle and searched the ground.

'What're you hunting, Clay?' Junior asked.

Clay spoke without looking up from the earth that was still damp and soft from melted snow. 'I'm wondering if anyone has been using our line shack this spring.'

'You mean rustlers,' Junior said.

Clay glanced at the kid, but did not reply.

'Talk in the bunkhouse,' Junior said, 'is that we'll get hit by rustlers again this year. Some of the hands say that's why you hired a bigger crew, and that every one of us had better be ready to fight.'

Clay straightened up in the saddle. 'I hired cowhands, not gunmen.'

'You can handle that forty-five of yours,' Junior said. 'I've seen you.' He patted the big Remington in his holster. 'And I can use mine.'

Clay met the kid's blank stare, wondering if his words were a promise of help, or a threat. He remembered the time in the horse barn when Junior had pulled that gun and aimed it at him. The look of hatred on Junior's face was something Clay couldn't forget.

Junior smiled.

Clay turned his horse to the north. No hoof prints were there. 'Let's go see how the roundup crews are doing.'

CHAPTER 12

Clay let his gelding pick a way through the Circle R cattle grazing near the roundup camp, and rode on to the branding corral. Reining up there, he threw a leg over the saddle horn, and watched Junior do the dusty, rough job he'd learned during the last week.

'Calf rassler,' he was called, and every time a cowhand riding a cutting horse brought a cow and her calf from the herd, Junior would open the corral. Hazed inside, the cow and calf were trapped when Junior closed the gate.

Clay watched as Junior leaped and lunged, at last catching the agile, wild-eyed calf. Wrestling it off its flailing feet, Junior and another cowhand dragged the calf to the men who waited at the branding fire.

The bawling calf sent his mother on the prod, her horns slashing and hooves kicking as she made short charges. While the cherry-red Circle R branding iron was pressed into young hide, other cowhands waved their hats in Mama's face, distracting her long enough for the deed to be done.

This calf was a male, and he was quickly

castrated by a cowhand wielding a pocket knife, then turned loose with his mother. Junior opened the corral gate, and both animals ran out, one bawling in pain and the other mooing at the indignity.

Clay was well satisfied. This week more than three thousand head of cattle had been driven to the holding ground. The branding fire had burned every day, and cows with calves had been run through the corral in a steady procession. The Circle R herd had grown, and even with the loss to rustlers last year, Clay would ship more four-year-old steers this fall than ever before.

As the cattle were tallied, they were gradually divided into manageable herds and driven northward to summer pasture. One afternoon in the second week of roundup, Clay rode with one of the herds as far as the home ranch. There he reported to the Old Man.

'Sounds good, Clay, real good,' Rawls said, grinning as he sat in his favorite chair in the main room of the ranch house. In the crook of one bony arm he held the sleeping infant.

Clay smiled, too, knowing that the Old Man was grinning more from the job of holding the child than he was from hearing about the condition of Circle R stock.

'Clay?'

He turned and saw Annie come out of her

room, rubbing sleep from her eyes. She pulled her robe around her slim body.

'Hello, Annie,' Clay said.

'I thought I heard your voice,' she said, smiling as she looked at him. 'How's round-up going?'

'Fine so far,' Clay said. He watched her come across the room, and added, 'You're looking well, Annie.'

'I'm getting my strength back,' she said. She moved to Rawls's side and put her hand on his shoulder, looking down at her baby.

'Does Jess ever let you hold him?' Clay asked.

She laughed softly. 'Once in a while.'

Rawls looked up at his foreman. 'Ever see such a good-looking boy, Clay? Ain't he something?'

'He is, at that,' Clay said, looking from the baby's face to Annie's. Their eyes met, and a moment of silence followed.

'Would you eat an early supper?' she asked. 'I can have something on the table pretty quick.'

Clay nodded. 'Be a pleasure to sit at a real table and eat food that doesn't have dust settling over it.'

Rawls chuckled. 'That's why I'm damn glad you're running the show these days, Clay. Spring roundup, that's work for young men who don't mind sleeping on the ground and eating dirt with son-of-a-bitch stew.

Many's the year I done that.' He glanced down at the sleeping baby. 'Now I can just sit back and take it easy.'

Clay shook his head, smiling. 'I'll get cleaned up for a proper meal, Annie.'

Outside he carried water from the creek and filled the tub in the bunkhouse. After a bath and a shave, he put on his first set of clean clothes in a week.

Clay and Annie sat alone at one end of the long mess table while the Old Man stayed in the other room with William. Little conversation passed between them, and as the mealtime wore on, Clay felt more and more uncomfortable.

Annie cast frequent glances at him, seemed on the verge of speaking, but when Clay looked straight at her, her face reddened.

'Well,' she blurted at last, 'how are all those cows?'

'Dumb as ever,' Clay said.

Annie cocked her head slightly. 'Cows are dumb?'

Clay nodded.

'Oh?' she said.

After another long moment Annie slapped her hand on the table top. 'Clay, I can't think of anything to talk to you about!'

Clay put down his fork and laughed. 'I'm having the same trouble. One time you said that all us men ever talk about is weather and stock and practical jokes. I've been sitting here trying to think of something to talk over, and coming up dry. Hell of a thing.'

'Oh, Clay,' she said. 'I shouldn't have said that. Sometimes words fall out of my mouth before I think.'

Clay shook his head. 'The worst of it was, it was the truth.' He added, 'You know, as much as we've been through together, we should have plenty to talk about.'

She raised a hand to her mouth. 'Now, I am embarrassed.'

'Why?' Clay asked.

'You know more about me...' Her soft voice trailed off. 'Well, I was thinking the other day that you know so much about me that you probably don't like me much.'

'What?' Clay asked in surprise.

'Familiarity breeds contempt, they say,' Annie said.

'Who the hell said that?' Clay asked.

She smiled and shrugged.

'What I know about you,' Clay said, 'is that you're one strong young woman. And a brave one.'

'You ... don't dislike me?' she asked.

Clay shook his head. 'Not even one little bit.'

In the next week the calf-branding was finished, the last of the tally recorded, and the cattle were drifted onto summer pastures by the cowhands. Roundup camp was dismantled, and Cookie returned to the home ranch.

Through all the calf-wrestling and other dirty jobs that always fell to the youngest hand on the ranch, Junior worked hard, without complaint. Clay began to think that he had judged the kid too harshly last year. Maybe the Old Man had been right. Junior needed time to grow up.

Clay had begun to doubt his judgment of Roy Long Knife, too. After two weeks, still no sign of him. Clay wondered if he'd been injured while breaking horses at the DHS. Or perhaps he'd returned to the Blackfoot Indian reservation after having second thought about working as an outrider on a ranch where trouble was expected.

But Clay's doubts were relieved two days later, in the dark of night. Awakened by a rough hand closing over his mouth, Clay tried to rear up from his bunk, lashing out with a fist.

'It's me,' came a voice in the darkness, and the man blocked Clay's blow with his forearm.

Clay peered through the blackness. Against the background of Cookie's steady snoring, he saw a shadowy figure standing over him, a figure he slowly recognized as Roy Long Knife.

'I found a man,' Roy said, taking his hand from Clay's mouth.

Clay sat up, not understanding. 'What?'

'A man's watching your cattle and riders,' Roy said. 'Rides alone, watches through a long spyglass.'

'Where is he?' Clay asked as his feet hit the floor.

'On a ridge by the north pasture,' Roy said. 'We can take him at dawn if we ride out now.' Roy left the cabin.

Clay pulled on his clothes and boots. He grabbed his Stetson off a peg by the door and went outside, strapping his gunbelt around his waist.

By faint starlight he saw two horses in the yard. Roy Long Knife waited there, mounted on his spotted horse. He held the reins of the second horse, and as Clay moved closer, he recognized his own gelding, saddled and bridled. Roy had planned ahead.

'Lead the way,' Clay said, taking his horse's reins and swinging up into the saddle.

Riding across the darkened grasslands beyond the valley of the ranch, Clay glanced up at the sky. He saw a vast black bowl pin-pointed with stars. The night was silent except for the sounds of loping horses, shod hooves striking the earth, and creaking saddle leather. Cool air breezed past Clay's face.

He'd had no idea of the time when he was awakened. But now Clay realized that they were several hours' ride away from the north pasture and that Roy intended to be there before the first light. The hour now had to be one or two in the morning, no later.

Stopping for a rest, Clay accepted a strip of elk jerky from Roy and bit off a chunk. He chewed vigorously, then took a mouthful of water from his canteen. The pungent meat swelled and softened in his mouth, and he chewed for several minutes before swallowing.

Riding again across the starlit land, Clay became absorbed in thought, and suddenly realized he had dozed in the saddle while his gelding steadily trailed Roy's spotted pony.

In the night sky Clay discovered Squaw Peak looming up ahead, blocking out stars on the horizon. Farther on, Roy turned and guided his pony down into the bottom of a dry ravine. Clay followed.

Roy reined up and dismounted. Clay did the same. Working silently, they loosened their saddle cinches and hobbled their horses.

'This way,' Roy whispered, and walked silently along the winding ravine as it angled north and east. A quarter of a mile away Roy rounded a bend and stopped. He dropped to his knees, motioning for Clay to sit.

Clay sat in the sandy bottom of the ravine. He peered ahead into the darkness faintly lighted by stars, but he saw nothing.

The stars in the sky gradually dimmed,

and after a time Clay made out a horse standing in the ravine bottom fifty yards away. The animal was asleep on its feet.

Roy pointed, and then Clay saw the camp. Set on a narrow shelf near the top of the ravine bank was a saddle and a pile of gear amid tall tufts of grass.

There, wrapped in a dark blanket, was the man. The pointed toes of his boots stuck out of one end of the blanket, and at the other end was his bare head, face turned away.

Roy gestured at Clay to wait there, then he pulled off his boots and walked silently down the ravine to the horse. Clay drew his revolver, watching the sleeping man. A random thought occurred to him: This could be the man who'd ambushed him last fall.

In a glance Clay saw Roy stroke the horse's nose and run a hand along the animal's back as he passed by it. The horse tossed his head, but made no sound. Clay breathed easier.

Climbing to the top of the bank, Roy drew his knife. He signaled Clay to move in.

Clay crossed the bottom of the ravine and made his way closer to the sleeping man. He climbed the soft dirt bank slowly, keeping a wary eye on him. When he reached the top, Clay moved closer, one slow step at a time.

Suddenly Clay froze as the man groaned in his sleep and rolled over, his eyes fluttering. From the other side, Roy swiftly stepped up to the man, drew his bare foot back, and kicked him in the side.

The man bellowed. He thrashed and struggled against the blanket twisted around him, reaching frantically to his waist.

'If you come up with a gun, mister,' Clay said, kneeling beside him, 'you're dead.'

The man stopped struggling. He stared angrily at the Colt .45 aimed at his face, and then he glared at Clay.

'Bring your hands out, slow and easy,' Clay said.

The man drew his arms out of the blanket. His hands were empty.

Roy reached down and yanked the blanket off him. The man had slept in his clothes. Tucked into the waistband of his trousers was a nickel-plated revolver with ivory grips. Roy took the gun from him.

'What the hell do you want?' The man asked. 'Money?'

'I'll ask the questions,' Clay said. 'Your job is to come up with the right answers. What's your name?'

'John Jones,' he replied.

'Sure,' Clay said, aiming his .45 at the man's right eye. 'Is that the name you want carved on your grave marker?'

The man's square face turned ashen. He glanced at the impassive Roy Long Knife, then looked back at Clay. 'You wouldn't gun a man down in cold blood...'

'After you tell me your real name,' Clay

said, 'I want to know what you're doing here, and why you're so damned interested in Circle R cattle.'

While Clay spoke, Roy picked up a pair of saddlebags and went through them. He pulled out a collapsed telescope, then found a short-handled branding iron and a pair of heavy gloves.

'Clay,' Roy said.

Clay looked at him. 'Well, look at that – a running iron. I reckon I don't need to ask any more questions.'

'Now, hold on!' the man exclaimed. 'You've got the wrong idea.' He took a breath. 'You men are Circle R riders, aren't you?'

'I'm getting the idea that you planned to alter some brands with that iron,' Clay said. 'Want to tell me what's wrong with my thinking?'

'Damn right, I will,' he said. 'I took that iron off some rustlers a couple weeks ago, over on the Lazy T. It's evidence. It's going to be used in court.'

'Good yarn,' Clay said.

'I can prove it!' he said, his voice rising in anger and frustration. 'My name's Elmer Larkin. I'm a range detective, hired by the Montana Stockgrowers Association. If you don't believe me, ask Jess Rawls.'

CHAPTER 13

The hot sun was high in the sky when Clay and Roy Long Knife brought Larkin to the home ranch. Clay had taken the precaution of tying the prisoner's hands behind his back, and he rode behind while Roy led Larkin's horse.

Elmer Larkin remained silent during the ride, but Clay noticed that his neck was bowed with anger.

Even though Larkin carried no identification papers, Clay realized that he might have been telling the truth. 'Too risky,' Larkin had said in explaining why he carried neither papers nor a badge identifying him as a stock detective. If he fell in with a gang of rustlers, he could claim that he was on the dodge himself.

But what could be more risky, Clay thought, than carrying a running iron in cattle country? The man's behavior didn't add up. From the ranch, Clay was prepared to take him into Yellow Pine where he would wire the county sheriff to come and get him.

They were met at the ranch house by the Old Man. He came out on the porch and stood at the edge, hands on his hips. Annie stepped into the doorway behind him, a worried look on her face.

'Where you been, Clay?' Rawls demanded. He looked at the other two men. 'What the hell's going on?'

Clay dismounted. 'We found this trespasser up in the north pasture. He was carrying a spyglass. And this.' Clay pulled the running iron out of Larkin's saddlebag.

'I'll be damned,' Rawls said.

'Mr Rawls, don't you remember me?' Larkin's voice was almost pleading.

The Old Man stepped off the porch and looked up at him, squinting against the noon sun. 'Do I know you, mister?'

'A week ago you were glad to see me,' Larkin said. 'I told you I was sent here to patrol Circle R range, and you said it was about time you got something for the dues you pay into the Stockgrowers Association. Don't you remember?'

'Are you that feller?' Rawls asked, studying him.

Larkin cast a triumphant glance at Clay.

Clay asked, 'You know this man, Jess?'

'A feller did come through about a week ago,' Rawls said, 'when you was down at the roundup camp. A stock detective, name of...' Rawls though for a moment, then looked down, shaking his head.

'Elmer Larkin,' Larkin said.

'Yeah, that sounds right,' Rawls said,

112

looking up at Clay. 'I told you about him.'

'No, you didn't,' Clay said evenly.

'Well, I meant to,' Rawls said. 'You sure I never told you?'

Clay nodded.

Rawls seemed confused. He slowly turned away and stepped up onto the porch. Moving across to the door, he said over his shoulder, 'Turn him loose, Clay.'

After Rawls had gone inside with Annie and closed the door, Clay stepped around Larkin's horse and untied the rope binding his hands.

'I owe you an apology,' Clay said.

Larkin vigorously rubbed his wrists as he glared down at Clay. 'Mister, I've got a good notion to knock your face in.'

'I wouldn't blame you for trying,' Clay said. 'But you won't have an easy time of it.'

They stared at one another for a long moment. Finally Larkin said, 'Damned poor treatment for a man who's trying to save you from losing another herd of cattle to rustlers.'

'You after the same gang?' Clay asked.

Larkin nodded. 'We've had reports of men leading a string of pack animals. Might be the gang that hit you last year.'

'I wish the Stockgrowers Association had sent a wire telling me that,' Clay said.

Larkin paused. 'Hell, I shouldn't be mad at you.' He looked at the ranch house, then to Clay. 'I can see what you're up against here. The Old Man's losing his marbles, ain't he?'

'Jess has his good days,' Clay said. 'And some not so good.'

'Well,' Larkin said, exhaling, 'let's just forget this whole damned thing.'

'I'm willing,' Clay said

Larkin examined his wrists, then took up the reins. 'I'm going to catch the next train to Great Falls. I was a fool to carry that running iron. I'll turn it over to district court for safe keeping, like I should have in the first place.'

'Let me know when you ride back this way,' Clay said with a lopsided grin.

Roy Long Knife moved beside the range detective's horse and returned the pickle-plated revolver to him.

Larkin thrust the gun into his waistband. 'You're damned right I will, Clay.' He turned his horse and rode away.

Clay went into the kitchen pantry and gathered up a sack of food for Roy Long Knife. After seeing the man off, he returned to the kitchen, poured himself a cup of coffee, and added sweetened condensed milk until the brew turned the colour of buckskin.

He sat at the long mess table and tried to eat cold beef with sourdough bread. Hungry as he was, the food went down hard.

Annie came in and sat across from him.

'What happened, Clay?'

'Damn near killed a man this morning,' he said. 'The wrong man.' He forced another bite down, took a drink of coffee, and then told her about the night ride and confrontation at dawn.

When he finished, Annie said, 'Clay, I'm worried about Jess. This morning he couldn't remember my name. He was upset because he couldn't find you. That was all he could think about.'

'Sometimes Jess gets confused,' Clay said. 'He'll come out of it after he's had some rest. Did he go back to bed?'

Annie nodded. 'He's had spells like this before?'

'Worse,' Clay said. 'Last August he drove his buggy out to a pasture and ordered the cowhands to move the herds south. Rawls told them winter was coming, and he didn't want the cattle caught in a blizzard.'

'Oh, no,' Annie whispered.

'Soon as I heard about it,' Clay said, 'I came in here and tried to find out what was going on. The Old Man didn't remember a thing. He was in a foul mood, and told me if I didn't do a proper job of ramrodding this outfit, he'd find a man who could.'

'I can't imagine him talking to you that way.' Annie said.

'Why do you say that?' Clay said. 'He's the boss.'

'You know what Jess told me after you got back?' Annie asked. 'He said, "Everything's all right now. Clay's back."'

The sound of the crying infant turned Annie's head. She stood, glanced at Clay, then left the kitchen.

Clay watched her go. Before she came here, he'd had no idea that the Old Man felt so dependent on him.

Saturday night Clay rode with the crew to Yellow Pine. Like the cowhands, he was eager to blow off steam. Spring roundup was behind him, and all the Circle R cattle had been moved to summer pasture. Clay had left a skeleton crew with the herds and turned the rest of the cowhands loose.

Clay's prediction about Rawls had been right. After sleeping most of the morning, the Old Man had walked out of his bedroom as though nothing out of the ordinary had happened. He cheerfully asked Annie about the baby, and then hollered at Cookie to fix him something to eat.

Over the town of Yellow Pine the Montana sky turned pale blue with streaks of orange as the sun sank into the western horizon. From a distance of a quarter of a mile Clay saw that the town had grown since the last time he was there on that Saturday night before spring roundup.

Tents and shacks sprawled across the flat

from Cottonwood Creek to the railroad tracks, and out into the grasslands on all sides. Even Dirty Gertie was prospering. As he rode past her low cabin three drunken men came out, singing.

Clay and Circle R riders splashed across the creek and rode up the opposite bank. The sounds of horses brought women out of their cribs on Four-bit Flats, and they called to the cowhands.

Riding on, Clay saw crowds of men on the boardwalks. Like bees on a hive, they moved in and out of the various tent stores, saloons, and gambling dens. All types of men were there, from well-dressed dandies to those who wore little more than rags and had probably ridden the rods of a freight car to get to this jumping-off place to the gold district.

Scattered in the crowds were construction workers and railroad men, and as Clay rode down the narrow main street, he saw the burly figure of Angus Macdougal walking along the boardwalk to the Bon Ton Saloon.

The largest building in Yellow Pine now was the warehouse that stood at the end of the railroad loading platform. Built of heavy planks with wide doors on rollers, it had a sign on the front: MAJESTIC MINING & MILLING COMPANY. On the rail siding nearby were half a dozen cars housing workers, and a hundred yards farther down the tracks were stacks of ties and a mound of gravel. Clay realized this was the beginning of the railroad spur to the gold district.

The Circle R riders reined up in front of the Bon Ton, dismounted, and tied their horses at the hitching rail. Most of the crew spread out to tour the tent businesses, claiming they were 'looking for the elephant.'

Clay crossed the boardwalk and entered the saloon. All the gaming tables were empty at this early hour, and only a few men stood at the bar. Among them was Angus Macdougal.

'Clay!' Frenchy called out. 'A long time I haven't seen you.'

'We've been working critters for the last couple of weeks,' Clay said as he crossed the room.

'You and all the other ranches in northern Montana,' Frenchy said. 'I could go broke.'

Clay grinned while he took a place at the bar beside Macdougal. 'With all the thirsty men in this town, you must be getting rich.'

Frenchy replied in despair. 'The gamblers and those girls in Four-bit Flats leave very little for me.'

Clay ordered a mug of beer and turned to Angus Macdougal. 'Evening, Mr Macdougal.'

The big foreman nodded hello. 'I remember meeting you last fall, Clay. Call me Gus.'

118

'Quite a warehouse you built, Gus,' Clay said. 'What're you working on now?'

Macdougal grimaced. 'Laying track to the mountains. Ain't good work. Have to keep after the men every damned minute.' He drank a long swallow of beer. 'Money. That's the only reason for working in this god-forsaken country.'

Clay cast a wink at Frenchy. 'Some of us like it.'

'Why sure,' Macdougal said. 'You skinny fellers on horseback look like you belong to this land. But try sitting in this damned tent town for a few weeks.'

'Could get slow,' Clay allowed.

'More 'n that,' Macdougal said. 'Keeping my crew sober and healthy is a job by itself. Two nights ago one of my men got himself knifed by a whore. Last Saturday a saloon fight put three of my workers down.'

'You've got your hands full,' Clay said, 'for a fact.'

'I have,' Macdougal grunted, drinking from his mug again. He banged the mug down on the bar top, and looked at Clay. 'Keep your damned cow chasers away from my men, and I'll be obliged.'

Clay was surprised and amused by the note of challenge in the man's voice. Clay met his steady gaze until the door of the saloon opened and slammed shut.

He turned and saw Henry Reid come in.

Strutting like a bantam rooster, the telegrapher came across the room, heading straight for Clay.

CHAPTER 14

Henry Reid elbowed his way to the bar between Clay and Angus Macdougal. He waved unnecessarily to catch the saloonkeeper's attention.

'Set up the bar, Frenchy,' Reid said.

'That's mighty generous of you Henry,' Clay said.

Reid grinned. 'Times are good, real good.' In a lower voice he added, 'I've got all my town lots rented out.'

'You haven't sold them?' Clay asked.

'No, no,' Reid said, and fell silent while Frenchy set mugs of foaming beer in front of them.

When the saloonkeeper moved away, Reid went on. 'The time isn't right for selling. Oh, I could have sold them a hundred times, for plenty more than what I paid. They're going up in price every week, but they're going to be worth plenty more when this gold boom takes hold. You watch. Majestic will build boarding houses, and other business will come in. We'll have schools, churches here, everything. Even a town marshal to keep the peace.'

'That's quite a vision of the future,' Clay said.

Reid nodded. 'I haven't given you a wrong steer yet, have I?'

'No,' Clay said, 'you haven't.'

Reid looked at him expectantly, obviously hoping Clay would express regret for not buying town lots when he'd had the chance.

Instead, Clay raised his beer mug at the telegrapher. 'Here's to the town builders, Henry.'

The saloon door banged open. A man dressed in dirty overalls rushed to Angus Macdougal's side.

'There's a fight outside, Gus!' he exclaimed. 'Between Sam Travis and one of those cow chasers.'

Macdougal growled, gulped down the beer Reid had bought, and slammed the mug down on the bar. He strode to the door with the construction worker trailing a step behind.

Reid said, 'I saw a fight brewing when I came in. In tent town a bunch of those construction boys were hoorawing cowhands.' He added, 'Some of your men were in on it, Clay.'

Clay studied the half-filled mug in front of him. He could have lived a happy life without hearing that. A moment later he tugged his Stetson down on his head and walked out of the saloon. Reid followed.

Down the rutted street Clay saw a large group of men gathered near the open space between Mays's General Store and a large tent that displayed a sign advertising mining supplies. The men were silent and still, and Clay knew before he got there that they were watching a fight.

Making his way through the crowd, Clay saw Curly squared off with a construction worker. As usual the feisty cowhand had taken on a man half again his size.

Both men were bloodied. Their jaws and foreheads were reddened from taking punches, and a smear of dirt on the construction worker's overalls indicated that he had been down. Cautious now, the two men moved slowly, fists raised, circling. As Clay watched, they alternately feinted, ducked, and snapped jabs at one another.

Angus Macdougal stood inside the circle of onlookers, and across the way stood Wash. With his big arms folded across his chest, the black cowhand looked on impassively.

Suddenly the construction worker faked a punch and shot his foot out, kicking Curly's knee. For a moment Curly was off-balance and the construction worker threw a roundhouse punch that landed squarely on his jaw.

Curly dropped to the ground like a sack of oats, and again the construction worker drew back his foot to kick Curly in the face. Wash swiftly moved behind the construction worker, threw his arms around him, and lifted him off his feet.

Several other men in Macdougal's crew rushed in to help their man, and they were met by a group of cowhands. Before a melee could start, Clay drew his revolver and fired it into the air.

The unexpected explosion brought a sudden stillness.

'The fight's over,' Clay said. 'Break it up, or the next shot won't be in the air.'

Several of the Circle R men raised a protest, and Zeb Hayes said, 'I had money riding on Curly, and he'd have won if that dirt digger had fought fair.'

'No holds barred!' shouted one of the construction workers.

An argument ensued, and the two groups squared off against each other. They stopped at the sound of Angus Macdougal's bellowing voice.

'Stop this fighting!' Macdougal shouted.

Slowly, the two groups backed away. Macdougal moved into the widening space. Curly was sitting on the ground dazed, and Wash still held the construction worker aloft.

Macdougal glanced around, then said to

Clay, 'Tell your black boy to let my man go.'

'He's a grown man,' Clay said evenly. 'Out here in Montana we don't call him "boy."'

'You know what I mean,' Macdougal said. He added, 'I'm trying to make peace around here.'

'Your man doesn't fight fair,' Clay said, 'and now you're calling a top hand "boy." That's a poor way to make peace.'

Macdougal stared angrily at Clay.

'Call him Mr Washington,' Clay said, 'and he'll let your man go. Then I want the money returned. All bets are off.'

A storm of protests and curses burst from the crowd of construction workers. The men gathered behind Macdougal, who in that moment became their spokesman.

'I ought to take you apart, cow chaser,' he said in a growling voice.

'With what?' Clay asked. 'A pick and shovel?'

Laughter came from the cowhands.

'My bare hands,' Macdougal said, his face coloring. 'Get rid of that gun, and we'll make this a fair fight.'

Clay met the Scotsman's angry glare, and he heard men call out on either side of him.

'Go to it, Clay.'

'Come on, Gus.'

'You throw him, and we'll geld him.'

'Take him, Gus, take him.'

Clay reached to his waist and unhooked his gunbelt. As he did so, Wash released the construction worker, and he helped Curly to his feet.

The two opposing groups of cowhands and construction workers suddenly lost their hostility and intermingled to make bets on the outcome of the fight. Clay saw Junior in the crowd, and he watched as the kid placed a bet with Henry Reid.

Bets laid, the two groups moved apart, leaving a space between them for the combatants.

Clay watched this happen as he handed his gunbelt to Bill Clark. How the hell did I get into *this*, he wondered, turning to face Macdougal. The big man was rolling up his sleeves, exposing brawny arms and battered knuckles.

'Come and get it, cow chaser,' Macdougal said, and a cheer went up from the construction workers.

This cheer was answered by another, louder yell from the gathered cowhands.

Hoping he was faster on his feet and more agile, Clay moved in quickly and hit Macdougal with a left to the face and a stiff right to the body, then slid away.

Macdougal grinned and came for him. Clay backpedaled, quickly sidestepped, and hit the man again this time squarely on the jaw. Pain shot through Clay's arm as the punch landed solidly, and the cowhands shouted in triumph.

More embarrassed than hurt, Macdougal lumbered after Clay, swinging with both hands. An unskilled fighter, he clearly relied on power.

Clay ducked a wild punch, and threw his right into Macdougal's thick midsection. But a moment later one of the man's big fists caught Clay high on the head. Clay was nearly knocked off his feet.

Stumbling to one side, Clay almost fell. He realized he'd never been hit so hard. Regaining his footing, he backed away. The crowd of men had fallen silent.

Clay backpedaled again, moving away from the advancing Macdougal. Solid punches to the face hadn't hurt the big foreman but had only angered him, like slapping a bull on the nose.

Clay had seen the man grimace when he'd slugged him in the midsection, though, and he watched for an opening to hit him there again.

As Macdougal closed, drawing back his right fist, Clay went low and put all his weight behind a punch to the stomach. He heard a groan as he drove his fist in, but as he moved away. Macdougal caught him with a blow to the side of his head.

Clay didn't remember falling, but suddenly dust was in his mouth, along with a faint taste of blood, and he rolled over on the ground, staring up at the sky. Cheers and shouts came into his hearing like the distant roar of a waterfall.

Wash jumped in between the two men. 'No kicking this time,' he said to Macdougal. None of the men challenged Wash, and Macdougal stepped back.

Clay rose to all fours and slowly got to his feet. He heard a cowhand say, 'This thing ain't over yet,' as he turned to face Macdougal.

Wash moved out of the way. Through a steady buzzing sound in Clay's ears came shouts of encouragement from the cowhands.

Legs heavy now, Clay knew he had lost some of his advantage. As Macdougal came toward him, Clay realized he somehow would have to change his strategy or it was all over.

Pretending to be more dazed than he was, Clay rocked back on his heels and did not jab or bob out of harm's way when Macdougal approached. The big foreman cocked his right arm back and threw a punch that he expected would end this fight as he must have ended many others.

But an instant before he would have been hit, Clay ducked down. Macdougal's fist whispered overhead, his momentum extending his body all the way around. Then Clay rose and buried his fist in the man's midsection.

Macdougal's face went slack as air rushed out of him. Clay hit him again in the belly, and Macdougal cried out, dropping his fists to protect himself.

With rapid punches, Clay tattooed Macdougal's face, and the moment Macdougal raised his hands Clay again hit him in the stomach. Groaning, Macdougal sank to his knees. Another punch to the temple toppled the big foreman. He lay on the ground, still.

'By God, Clay, you dropped him like a tree,' Zeb Hayes said excitedly.

Chest heaving, Clay bent over with his hands on his knees. Cowhands shouted their congratulations, but Clay knew that luck had turned the fight. He was lucky to have been able to stand after Macdougal had nearly brained him with a punch that would have knocked a brick out of a wall, and he was lucky to have found the man's vulnerable spot. For some reason, a blow to the midsection brought paralyzing pain to Macdougal.

Bets were collected, and the construction workers revived their foreman and helped him to his feet. Leaning against men on either side of him, Macdougal hobbled away without looking back.

Clay walked with his Circle R riders and other cowhands back to the Bon Ton Saloon.

The men were in a celebrating mood, promising to buy Clay as much beer as he could drink.

Henry Reid moved in front of Clay, walking fast to stay ahead. He held up two twenty-dollar gold pieces. 'That first beer you drink will be mine, Clay. I put money on you to whip that Scotsman, at two-to-one odds.'

Clay nodded, realizing then that Junior had bet against him.

CHAPTER 15

'Last winter you said you'd show me the Circle R,' Annie said. 'Every square foot of it.'

Clay looked at her and saw her smile as though she knew a secret. In the cool of this Sunday evening they sat together on the porch of the ranch house, with the baby asleep in his rocker between them.

'When did I say that?' Clay asked.

Annie slowly rocked the baby. 'When you were flat on your back, recovering from the gunshot wound.'

'Must have been out of my head,' Clay said.

She smiled again. 'You were groggy. But

you were grateful that I was caring for you. You even liked my singing.'

'That proves I was out of my head,' Clay said.

Annie laughed.

'What else did I say to you?' he asked.

She shrugged, suddenly shy. 'Not much.'

Clay took a long look at her. 'Pack a lunch tomorrow. I'll show you every square foot of the north pasture.' He glanced down at the sleeping infant. 'What about Mr William J Davenport?'

'I'll leave him with Jess,' Annie said.

'Sure that's a good idea?' Clay asked. 'We'll be gone all day.'

'Cookie will keep an eye on them both,' she said easily.

'Sounds like you've already got this planned out with Cookie,' Clay said.

Annie smiled.

The sky was cloudless and the mid-morning sun warmed the air as Clay drove the buggy out of the grass-laden valley of the Circle R home ranch and headed north toward the Bar Paw mountains. Annie sat on the tufted seat beside him. At her feet was a wooden box containing food and a quart jar of lemonade.

Topping the rise, they got a long view in all directions of rolling grasslands, freshly greened.

'The land seems endless,' Annie said, looking around. 'It's kind of scary and lonely, isn't it?'

Clay nodded as he drove along the crest of the rise. 'To survive out here you have to respect the land. You can't ever forget that nature is stronger than you are, and without mercy.'

Annie wore a cotton dress with a flower pattern, one that she had made last winter. The bodice gathered tightly under her breasts, and flared at her rounded hips.

Clay looked at the profile of her face. The line of her small nose and curving lips was lovely. And as she turned to look at him, her eyes were bright.

He again thought of the day when he'd first seen her. She had seemed to be such a helpless creature, totally out of her element. Now she was tanned and stronger, more self-assured. She smiled openly at him.

Clay turned the horse and let the animal pick his way down slope away from the valley. Not following any track, they traveled in a northerly direction all morning.

The sun was directly overhead when he stopped at a creek. The horse drank the clear water that slid over shiny stones and sand.

'The mountains are beautiful,' Annie said as Clay helped her out of the buggy. 'Look at the highest one. Snow is on top.'

Clay heard a note of delight in her voice as

she made the discovery. 'Squaw Peak,' he said, looking up at the towering mountain of gray granite.

'Just think of the view from the top of that mountain,' she said. She turned to him, her eyes sparkling. 'Wouldn't it be wonderful?'

Clay nodded. 'Someday we'll ride horse-back on the old Blackfoot Indian trail–'

As he spoke, his eye was caught by the flowing stream at his feet. Water that was clear a moment ago now was clouded with mud the color of coffee and cream.

Annie noticed it, too. 'Clay, what caused that?'

'Animals crossing upstream, maybe,' he replied. 'Or a herd of cattle.' But as he watched, the water grew darker with mud, and then an empty sack of plug tobacco floated past.

'I'd better have a look,' Clay said.

They climbed into the buggy and Clay turned the horse upstream. The creek angled toward its snowy headwaters high in the Bear Paw mountains. From there it flowed into the grasslands and eventually on to Cottonwood Creek. The course of the creek here was between two gently sloping hills.

Clay drove beside the creek for a quarter of an hour. The water was still running mud. He rounded a bend and quickly reined up. Three horses and two pack animals were grazing in the high grass. On top of the hill sat a bearded man. He aimed a shotgun at them.

'Stop right there, mister,' he said. 'Get out of that rig, and keep your hands high. You, too, girlie. Move!'

The man wore knee-high rubber boots over his trousers, a flannel shirt, and a black felt hat with a wide brim.

Clay nodded at Annie. He climbed out of the buggy, hands raised, and she got out on the other side. She came around and stood beside him.

'Drop that gunbelt,' the man ordered.

Clay unhooked his cartridge belt. Letting the holstered revolver fall into the high grass, he felt stupid for driving into this trap. Last winter he'd been ambushed when he had followed a creek bottom instead of riding the high ground. Now he wondered if this could be the man who had shot him.

The man stood and came striding down the slope to the buggy. Training the shotgun on Clay, he looked into the buggy.

'What's in the box?' he demanded.

'Lunch,' Clay said. 'Have a look.'

The man grinned, showing missing teeth. 'Lift it out of there, mister.'

'You're trespassing on Circle R land–' Clay began.

The man jabbed the barrel of the shotgun at Clay's middle. 'Fetch that box. Walk upstream. You, too, girlie.'

Clay lifted the box out of the buggy, then walked along the bank of the stream, rounding the bend. Annie stayed close beside him, and the man with the shotgun followed. Ahead, Clay saw what he should have suspected from the first.

Standing in the stream were two prospectors shoveling sand out of the stream bed into a long sluice box. Water running through the box washed sand and dirt into the stream. Caught on a series of raised cross-pieces were heavier stones and possibly gold nuggets.

'Well, now, look what Zeke brung to us.'

The men stopped working and straightened up. Both wore rubber boots, and were dressed like the first man. They were bearded too, and one man wore a dark patch over one eye.

'A box of grub,' Zeke called out to them. 'And a woman.'

The two prospectors tossed their shovels into the sluice box and waded out of the stream to the bank.

'You're muddying water that belongs to the owner of the Circle R ranch,' Clay said.

Zeke punched Clay in the back with the barrel of the shotgun.

The biggest of the two prospectors who had been working in the stream was a round-shouldered, black-bearded man. He put his hands on his hips and faced Clay.

'Mr Cowman, we don't care who the hell owns this land. We're just passing through. We'll work this stream 'til we find colour. If we pick up nuggets here, we'll work our way to the mountains yonder to the vein. When we find that gold, we'll be so damned rich we can buy all the ranches in Montana, and cowmen like you will be dancing to our music.'

The prospector wearing a patch over his eye chuckled. He moved closer to Annie, reached out, and laid his hand on her breast.

Clay threw the box at the black-bearded prospector and lunged for the man wearing the patch. He got a hand on the man, but then his feet went out from under him as Zeke stuck the shotgun in his feet and tripped him.

Clay scrambled to his feet, and again went after the prospector who had touched Annie, but in the next instant the shotgun boomed.

'Mister, I'll blow you in half where you stand!' Zeke shouted.

Clay stopped.

The black-bearded prospector had been knocked to his knees by the lunch box. Now he got up. 'You should have done that in the first place, Zeke.'

'I couldn't without spraying everybody,' he said.

Clay sensed a weakness in Zeke's voice

135

and turned to face him. 'Kill a man? You ever done that before?' Clay stared at him until he looked away. 'Kill me,' Clay said, 'and you'll see my face every night before you sleep.'

'I won't,' the man wearing the eye patch said. Zeke did not raise his gaze to meet Clay's.

'Tie him up,' the black-bearded man said. 'Tie them both up. All we need is a few days to work this crick, then we'll move along.'

'We'll be missed in an hour,' Clay said. 'Every Circle R rider will come looking for us.'

The black-bearded prospector studied the contents of the spilled lunch box. 'That ain't likely.' He thought a moment. 'There's enough little gullies around here to keep an army busy. Now sit over there, and put your hands behind your back.'

Clay looked at Annie and nodded. Her expression was tight, but she showed no signs of fear. They sat together in the high grass while Zeke passed the shotgun to the black-bearded man. Zeke found two lengths of wire, and he used them to bind Clay's hands and then Annie's.

Clay watched the men explore the food that had fallen out of the lunch box. They hungrily ate the sandwiches and deviled eggs, and wolfed down an iced cake Annie had made last night.

The prospector with the eye patch licked sugar icing off his fingers. 'I bet the girlie's as sweet as this cake,' he said. 'And I bet we'll be finding out afore long.'

The other two prospectors chuckled. Clay strained frantically against the wire that bound his wrists.

CHAPTER 16

The afternoon dragged by while Clay watched the prospectors shovel rocks and sand into their sluice box. He twisted his wrists against the wire that bound him until his hands were wet and he knew he was bleeding.

All this time Annie sat in the grass with her head bowed. She had not cried or said a word all afternoon. Clay realized she was determined to never give these men the satisfaction of seeing fear in her.

One of the three prospectors was always resting as they took turns with sentry duty on the crest of the hill overlooking the grazing horses. The work was hard. Standing in cold water and lifting shovelfuls of wet sand and stones hour after hour required a strong back.

At sundown the men quit. As far as Clay

had seen, they had not found a single gold nugget, and they were in a foul mood. Sitting on the creek bank, they opened cans of beans and ate without building a fire.

Afterward, they talked in low voices, glancing back at Annie. They argued briefly, and then the black-bearded prospector tossed a silver dollar into the air.

'Ha!' shouted the prospector who wore a patch over one eye. He yanked off his rubber boots, stood, and came striding through the grass toward Annie.

'Now, I'm ready for something sweet,' he said, grinning. 'And warm.'

'I'm next,' the black-bearded man called after him. 'Don't forget that.'

Clay said to the one-eyed man, 'Get away from her.'

'You talk hard, mister,' he said, standing over Annie. 'If I was in your place, I'd be trying real hard to make friends about this time. You'd stay healthy if you told this girlie to be nice to us gentlemen. Get my meaning?'

'Lay a hand on her,' Clay said, 'and I'll see that you don't live to brag about it.'

The one-eyed man drew his bare foot back and kicked Clay in the chest.

'No!' Annie shrieked.

Clay was rocked back, but when he got his breath and sat up he said hoarsely, 'Cut me loose, and we'll settle this man to man.

Winner takes all.'

'I ain't got time for you, mister,' he said. Moving behind Annie, he reached down and pulled her to her feet.

'Don't take all damned night,' the black-bearded man said.

Watching Annie dragged away by the burly prospector Clay yanked against the wire again, but succeeded only in deepening his raw wounds. He lost sight of them when the prospector took Annie around the bend where the horse and buggy had been left.

A moment after Clay lost sight of them, he heard a strange sound, followed by a curse and deep moan. The one-eyed prospector came staggering around the bend, holding his stomach with both hands. Bright red blood stained his shirt front.

Both Zeke and the black-bearded prospector leaped to their feet, staring wide-eyed at the wounded man who stumbled toward them.

Clay glimpsed a thrown object flying through the air, and in the next instant a knife was embedded deep in the thigh of the black-bearded man. He cried out and went down, clutching his leg.

Zeke dove for the shotgun, but before he reached it, a rifle shot boomed. Dirt blossomed in the grass in front of Zeke. Rising to his knees, he thrust his hands straight up.

'Don't kill me! Don't kill me!'

Clay looked toward the bend in the stream. Roy Long Knife stepped into view, carrying the Winchester Clay had loaned him.

Roy moved to the writhing prospector and jerked the knife out of his thigh. The black-bearded man cried out again. After wiping the bloody blade on his trouser leg, Roy shoved the knife back into the sheath on his belt. Then he pushed Zeke to the ground with one foot.

'Stay there,' he said.

'Annie–' Clay began.

Roy turned and came to him. 'She's all right.' He leaned behind Clay and unbound the wire around his wrists.

Clay lunged to his feet and ran on stiffened legs to the creek bank and rounded the bend. There, near the grazing horses, he saw Annie slumped down in the high grass.

Clay rushed to her. Her wrists were still bound, and Clay loosened and removed the wire with his numbed fingers.

'Oh, Clay,' Annie whispered, wrapping her arms around his neck.

Clay embraced her and held her tightly against his chest.

'Thank goodness you're here,' she said, sobbing now.

'Thank Roy Long Knife,' Clay said.

After a long moment, she pulled away and looked into his eyes. 'I was so scared ... too scared to do anything...'

'You did fine,' Clay said. He stood and helped her to her feet.

'You're hurt!' she exclaimed when she saw his bleedings wrists.

'No, I'm all right,' he said. 'Come on.' He took her by the hand and they walked back to the buggy. Clay helped her into the rig, then picked up his gunbelt and revolver from the grass and buckled it around his waist.

Clay walked back around the bend where Roy stood over the prospectors. He held the Winchester in the crook of his arm. The black-bearded prospector steadily cursed him.

'Murdering savage … bastard … murderer…'

'I owe you, Roy,' Clay said, stepping up beside him. 'Thanks.'

Roy Long Knife nodded in reply. 'I sighted this bunch last evening from a mile away. Didn't know what they were up to until this morning when I got in close enough to see them set up that sluice box. I rode out for the ranch to get you when I heard a shotgun blast. Figured I'd better come back, and that's when I saw they had you and Annie. I crawled on my belly through the grass all afternoon, trying to figure out how to take them. When that sentry left to eat supper, I moved in close. Then one of them brought Annie to me.'

141

'Murdering bastards...' the black-bearded prospector said, groaning.

Clay nudged him sharply with the toe of his boot. 'You're damned lucky we're not.'

He looked up at Clay, a pleading look in his eyes. 'I'm bleeding to death.'

'You've got some time,' Clay said. 'You're one-eyed friend is the one you'd better be worrying about.'

The prospector with the patch over his eye lay curled in the grass, grasping his belly with both hands. He made no sound, except for his ragged breathing.

Clay turned to Zeke who knelt on the ground, staring at Roy Long Knife in fear. 'Go saddle your horses and bring them.'

Zeke continued staring at Roy, as though in a trance.

'Now!' Clay ordered.

Zeke blinked, looked at Clay, and then scrambled to his feet.

As the prospector stumbled away, Clay said, 'Better keep an eye on him, Roy. He's likely to hightail it.'

As Roy walked away, Clay stooped down and picked up the shotgun. He broke it open and took out the one remaining live shell. Shoving it into his pocket, Clay turned and threw the weapon into the grass far upstream.

Clay waded into the cold water of the stream. He made his way over stones and through a patch of gleaming sand to the sluice box. Using one of the shovels as a pry tool, he dismantled the box. The boards floated slowly downstream as he pulled them apart. After tossing the two shovels onto the bank, Clay waded out of the water just as Zeke came back. He led the three saddle horses, followed by Roy.

Clay helped Zeke lift the one-eyed prospector into the saddle of one of the horses. The man slumped forward, but he grabbed the horn and stayed on.

Clay moved to the black-bearded prospector and pulled the man to his feet.

'Listen to me, mister,' Clay said in a voice scarcely louder than a whisper, 'and listen good. Get off Circle R land. Stay off this range, or you'll be buried here. I'll dig your grave myself. Hear me?'

The prospector did not look into Clay's eyes, but he nodded.

'What?' Clay shouted into his face.

'For God's sake,' he said, 'I hear you.'

Clay motioned for Zeke, and the two of them hoisted the big man into his saddle.

'Mount up,' Clay said to Zeke, 'and get out of here. All of you.'

At the home ranch Clay's wrists were bandaged by Cookie. The time was past midnight, and by lamplight in the kitchen Clay's wounds were washed and doctored. He and

Annie had told the Old Man what had happened that day.

Rawls was enraged at first, telling Clay that the prospectors should've been brought in. Later he calmed down when Annie assured him that she was all right.

Now, holding her baby, she watched Cookie bandage Clay's cut wrists.

Outside the kitchen door Roy Long Knife sat on his haunches and ate a late supper. After he finished, he set the tin plate and cup on the stoop and leaned into the doorway.

'I'll draw my wages,' he said.

Lamplight spilled through the back door and moths fluttered there. Clay stood when Cookie finished, and stepped outside.

'I'd like you to stay,' he said.

Roy shook his head. 'If word gets around that a half-breed drew blood from white men, they'll ride after me.'

'And you'll have the protection of every man on this ranch,' Clay said.

'I can't afford trouble,' Roy said. 'Too much of that on my back trail.'

Clay studied the man's face by lamplight. The dark hint about his past made him realize Roy must be a wanted man.

'All right,' Clay said at last. 'I'll get your wages.' As he stepped back into the kitchen, he said to Annie, 'Roy's leaving.'

The Old Man had gone back to bed. Clay

went to his desk in the main room of the ranch house. He found the cash box beneath a stack of papers and opened it. He counted out coins and then went back outside through the kitchen. Cookie held the sleeping baby, and in the doorway Annie was hugging Roy.

Embarrassed, Roy stepped back when he saw Clay. Clay grinned at him, and held out his hand. When Roy extended his, Clay dropped five twenty-dollar gold pieces into it.

'Too much,' Roy said in surprise.

'You earned it,' Clay said. 'And more. I want you to keep that Winchester.'

Roy started to protest, but as he met Clay's gaze, he nodded.

'Anytime you're looking for work,' Clay said, 'come here first.' He added, 'If a lawman comes through here asking questions about our go-round with those prospectors, I'll tell my side of the story. But I won't know your name.'

Roy Long Knife nodded his thanks and then turned and walked away, quickly disappearing in the darkness.

CHAPTER 17

In the next ten days Rawls made two trips to Yellow Pine to send and receive messages by telegraph. Clay didn't know the nature of these messages and, in talking to Annie, discovered that the Old Man had been secretive about it.

One evening Rawls said to Clay, 'We're getting such a crowd of people in this country now, that I reckon we'll have to run more trespassers off ever' year. Folks are saying Yaller Pine will grow into a city. I can believe it.'

'A tent town is a long way from a city, Jess,' Clay said.

'Yeah, I know,' he said, 'but it's growing. A man's got to look ahead, and I don't much like what I see. I liked the old days when this country was wild and the winters wasn't so blamed cold.' He paused and muttered, 'Damned gold boom, anyhow.'

'God booms have a way of going bust,' Clay said.

Rawls nodded absently, still absorbed in his thoughts of doom.

Clay changed the subject. 'I'm more worried about rustlers than prospectors or common trespassers. Beef is high-priced now. A gang of rustlers could hurt us – hurt us bad.'

'I know you're right, Clay,' Rawls said slowly. 'I get so damned tired now that I can't hardly think things out.'

Clay looked at the Old Man as he said this, and felt a tug deep inside. The remark was a sad confession from a proud man. 'The Circle R is in good shape, Jess, and I aim to keep it that way.'

Rawls smiled at him. 'Hell, I know you will, Clay.'

In the evening a rider from the Lazy T arrived in time for supper. He brought a message. The haying crew would be there day after tomorrow.

Spring and early summer this year had made an ideal growing season. Circle R meadows in the long valley along Cottonwood Creek were laden with the best crop of grass Clay had seen in the five years he'd been there.

On the porch of the ranch house he sat with Annie and the Old Man. They watched the high grass waving with an evening breeze. The sight was peaceful and satisfying, and no one spoke. Clay knew that when this year's crop was cut and baled, there would be more haystacks than ever.

In anticipation of the haying crew's arrival, Cookie and Annie had prepared food ahead.

They baked extra loaves of bread, churned butter, hard-boiled dozens of eggs, and made a trip to town to buy a large supply of canned fruit. And Clay ordered two Circle R steers slaughtered.

The same haying crew worked all the cattle ranches of northern Montana, having made their way from the earlier growing seasons to the south. In addition to a salary for each man, Clay was responsible for providing board and room. Extra cots were set up in the bunkhouse, and a long mess table was put in the shade of the front porch.

Partly to make room for the haying crew, and partly to fill the void left by Roy Long Knife, Clay established a new camp in the northern sector of the ranch. A tent was pitched near a tributary to Cottonwood Creek, and two riders were assigned to it on a rotating basis as on the winter line camps.

The riders were instructed to keep track of the cattle in the north pasture. This meant increased surveillance, in addition to the cowhands who normally traveled between the north sector and the home ranch, camping out for days at a time.

The camp was supplied by Specs. He made regular runs in the buckboard, and reported back to Clay to relay any messages. The riders based at the camp not only tended stock, but were alert for trespassers.

In the weeks after the haying season

several strangers were discovered on Circle R range. Most were innocent trespassers, along with a few unlucky prospectors. They were all eager to depart after being severely questioned and invited to move along by well-armed cowhands on horseback.

From the time the stock detective, Elmer Larkin, had ridden away from the ranch, Clay had received no word about rustlers from the Montana Stockgrowers Association.

He finally sent a request for information, and later the same week word came from a passing DHS rider that a message awaited him at the telegraph office.

Clay rode to town, passing Dirty Gertie's and splashing across Cottonwood Creek. On the opposite bank where the cribs of Four-bit Flats had stood, Clay was surprised to see bare ground. Farther on, he saw that most of the tent town was gone, too, and the railroad cars housing workers no longer stood on the siding by the loading pens.

Clay rode down the rutted street between the Bon Ton and Mays's General Store & Post Office, and on to the end of the street. He tied his gelding at the rail in front of the telegraph office. Dismounting, he climbed up onto the loading platform. At the open door of the telegraph office he was greeted with unexpected enthusiasm by Henry Reid.

'Been a long spell since I've seen you, Clay!' he said.

'This town's a little quieter than it was last time I was here,' Clay said, crossing the loading platform to the doorway of Reid's office.

'The rail spur hit the mountains last week,' Reid said, backing into his office as Clay entered. 'Tent town moved up there in a hurry.'

Reid moved around behind his desk. 'It's all for the best. The undesirable elements are gone from Yellow Pine now, and we can start building a real town. Mark my words, Clay. It's going to happen sooner than anybody thinks. The boom town will be in the mountains, but Yellow Pine will be the supply center for the whole mining district. And in the winter, everybody will move down here. If that doesn't bring year-around prosperity, I don't know what will.'

Clay realized Reid was no longer thinking only in terms of land investments. He made no mention of making quick profits on his town lots. Now he was a town builder.

The telegrapher pulled an envelope from a clip attached to a board over his desk. He handed the envelope to Clay.

Opening it, Clay took out the paper, unfolded it, and read the message.

REGARDING YOUR INQUIRY, DEPUTIZED

RANGE DETECTIVES HAVE BEEN OCCU-
PIED IN THEIR PURSUIT OF SUSPECTED
OUTLAWS SOUTH OF THE DHS RANCH
PROPERTY. UPON COMPLETION OF THEIR
MISSION. DETECTIVES WILL RETURN TO
CIRCLE R AND LAZY T RANGES FOR
PATROL DUTY. REPORT SUSPICIOUS TRES-
PASSERS ON YOUR RANGE TO THIS OFFICE
AT ONCE.

'Sending back a reply?' Reid asked.

Clay shook his head. Outside he untied his horse and led the animal down the street to the Bon Ton Saloon. He went in and drank a beer alone with Frenchy.

Frenchy was just as glad the boom town had moved on, too, Clay learned. Fights involving knifings and shootings had become nightly occurrences in the saloon, and Frenchy realized it was just a matter of time before some wild-eyed drunk came after him.

'The man who breaks up a fight is in the greatest peril,' the saloonkeeper said. 'Often both fighters would turn on me.'

Clay nodded remembering some of the bunkhouse brawls he'd broken up. 'Nobody likes a peacemaker.'

'Ah, but your cowhands are my good customers, Clay,' Frenchy said. 'Cowhands I know, I understand. They drink on Saturday night, tell lies, argue, shout, and fall asleep in their saddle on the way home. Those men I like. They do not carry knives or shiny little sneak guns, and they do not rob one another.'

Clay chuckled at Frenchy's analysis. After he finished the beer, he said, 'Henry Reid still thinks we've got the makings of a town here.'

'Al Mays believes so, too,' Frenchy said. 'Between them, those two own most of Yellow Pine. They believe they are town fathers.'

'What do you believe?' Clay asked.

Frenchy smiled. 'No one but a madman knows the future, Clay.'

Clay laughed. Frenchy had a way of putting his finger on the truth without revealing his own thoughts, at least not in a direct way.

In the evening after supper Clay walked with Annie to the corrals beyond the log horse barn. They stopped at one and watched a mare with her newborn filly. The filly had a sleek golden coat, and she stood close to her mother. With her large brown eyes and twitching ears, the filly looked out at the world beyond the safety of the corral.

'A miracle, isn't it, Clay,' Annie murmured. 'New life.'

Clay nodded. 'A newborn will stop a man in his tracks.' He leaned against the top pole of the corral. 'Stop and stare just like we're doing.'

They watched the mare nuzzle her filly while the evening light grew pale, then strolled back toward the ranch house. Ahead, seated on the porch, the Old Man sat holding the baby in his arms.

'Talk about miracles,' Clay said, jerking his head toward the ranch house, 'that baby of yours has given Jess something to live for, something he doesn't find on this ranch anymore.'

A moment later Clay heard the buckboard coming. He turned quickly. Specs was driving the team hard, and that wasn't like him.

'Clay!' Specs yelled as the running team came into the yard. 'Clay!'

Clay hurried to him.

'Shooting ... there's been a hell of a shooting!' Specs shouted, bringing the horses to a halt. He was short of breath and talking faster than Clay had ever heard him. 'Up in the north pasture camp... Bill Clark and Zeb Hayes ... shot to ribbons... Clay, they're dead!'

CHAPTER 18

Clay led the way across the darkening land, the thundering hooves of fourteen horses breaking the night silence behind him. He had rousted the cowhands out of the bunkhouse, sending a man on a fast horse to Yellow Pine where one message would be wired to the county sheriff and another to the Stockgrowers Association.

The armed cowhands reached the camp before midnight. Beside the gurgling creek Clay saw the tent and two corpses bathed in the frost-white light of half a moon. Lying where they had fallen, the murdered cowhands were sprawled in awkward positions, legs folded back, an arm twisted the wrong way, both men clutching their revolvers.

Tired as he'd been, Specs had insisted on coming, and had saddled a horse. Now when Clay reined to a halt, the lanky, bespectacled cowhand rode up beside him.

'See any tracks when you found them?' Clay asked.

'No,' Specs said, his voice thick. 'Not a one. Our boys was ambushed, Clay, pure and simple.'

Clay turned in his saddle and looked back

at the cowhands bunched behind him. Junior was in the lead, his eyes bright in the moonlight. He'd made the long night ride without hesitation, and now he looked like he was ready for more.

Behind Junior were Curly and Wash, along with nine others, all staring intently at Clay.

'Break out your shovels and light the lanterns,' Clay said. 'We'll dig graves for Bill and Zeb, and then get some rest. Soon as day breaks, we'll ride out and check the herds. By tracking cattle, I've got a hunch we'll run these killers down.'

Shortly before dawn the rider Clay had sent to Yellow Pine caught up, and according to plan the cowhand brought with him a pair of pack horses with panniers loaded by Cookie.

A fire was built, and by the time the eastern skyline was streaked with orange light Clay had made coffee from creek water. Two of the cowhands fried a breakfast of beefsteak and eggs on two large spiders – blackened iron skillets that stood on metal legs over the leaping flames.

Clay had slept little that night. Sounds of shovels stabbing into the earth and the silent burial by the cold light of the half moon had haunted his mind. The others must have felt the same, for now in the morning Clay sensed that the cowhands' tempers were on a hard edge. A mood of angry determination charged the air like an approaching storm.

After the men saddled their horses and topped them off, Clay divided the cowhands into three groups. He sent them to different sections of the north pasture, with instructions to report back in two hours whether they had found anything or not.

In less than two hours all three groups had returned. The signs were unmistakable. A hundred or more cattle had been driven out of the north pasture. Mixed in with those tracks were the hoof prints of half a dozen horses. Their trail led south, through hills that shouldered against the Bear Paws.

Clay followed the rustlers' trail all day, leading the men at a fast pace along the rolling hills above the flat grasslands. He was as certain as he could be that the cattle were bound for the new tent town at the end of the railroad spur. Somewhere nearby they would be butchered as quickly as possible, and the hides buried.

By evening Clay saw fresh cow manure amid the tracks. He slowed the pace, fearing they might blunder onto the thieves.

At full dark, Clay halted at a small spring. The pool of water reflected starlight, and the horizon beyond was obscured by a hill higher than the others. The cowhands made camp without building a fire or lighting a lantern, and ate from the cans of food Cookie had packed in the panniers.

Clay slept a hard, dreamless sleep that night. At the first light of day he was on his feet, awakening the cowhands wrapped in their blankets around the spring.

The men ate a cold breakfast of beans and hard bread. Each man was silent, keeping to himself. All of them knew that today they would catch the herd – and confront the thieves.

'Check your weapons,' Clay said, after they had finished eating and had filled their canteens from the spring.

Junior was the first to yank his gun out of his holster. The long-barreled Remington gleamed dully in the morning light as Junior looked at the bullets in the cylinder.

'We'll take it slow this morning,' Clay said, holstering his .45, 'and hope to hell we catch sight of them before they see us.'

They mounted their horses. Clay led the way up the steep and high hill to the south. He slowed as he reached the crest. Looking over the top, he saw a series of smaller hills, radiating away from the Bear Paw mountains like the folds of a huge blanket carelessly tossed to the earth. Far ahead, almost out of sight, Clay saw a dark, slowly moving mass – cattle.

Quickly halting, Clay signaled the riders to come ahead just far enough to see over the top.

'There they are!' Junior exclaimed.

The others were silent until Curly muttered, 'Damn, we camped five, six miles away from them last night, no more.'

'Good thing we didn't build a fire,' Wash added.

Clay scanned the terrain. To the east, where the hills gradually flattened into a vast, grassy plain, a dry gully angled southward.

'What're you figuring, Clay?' Specs asked.

'If those rustlers have any sense at all,' he replied, looking back at the cowhands, 'they're followed by a rear guard. Maybe two or three men with rifles and field glasses.'

'We've got them outnumbered,' Junior said. 'We can take them.'

Curly shook his head. 'They'll shoot us to pieces if we ride into them.'

Clay pointed to the east. 'See that dry wash? We'll backtrack and ride out there. Riding in the bottom of that wash will slow us down, but we can follow the herd and stay out of sight at the same time.'

Turning his horse, Clay rode back down the hillside, leading the men past the spring where they had camped last night. He led the way downslope out to the gully, just now realizing this was the southern end of the same dry wash that he and Roy Long Knife had followed to the stock detective's camp. In early spring, this sandy cut in the land carried runoff from melting snows, but was dry the rest of the year.

Clay let his gelding pick his way down the soft bank to the bottom, then turned the animal south. The Circle R riders strung out behind him. He had been right. Soft footing here made for slow going. But even so, Clay knew they could hold a faster pace than rustlers driving a herd of cattle.

The gully narrowed and deepened for a mile or more, then widened and became shallow for several miles, and finally deepened again as it meandered to the south along the foothills of the Bear Paws.

Under a hot noon sun Clay signaled a halt, and the cowhands silently ate another meal out of cans. From the bottom of one of the panniers someone discovered three quart bottles of beer. These were opened and passed around, each man taking long swallows of the warm brew.

At midafternoon they reached a grove of cottonwood trees. Here the gully flattened out to a wide, sandy wash, and beyond the trees was no concealment from the hills.

In the cool shade of the trees Clay dismounted. He was followed by the others. The men gathered around him, all of them scanning the foothills for movement or rising dust. They saw nothing.

'Maybe we're ahead of the bastards,' Curly said.

Clay nodded. 'Could be.'

Between this stand of cottonwoods and

the foothills was a mile or more of open ground, slanting up toward the hills.

'We can't take them by surprise from here,' Junior said. None of the cowhands replied, and Junior added, 'If we wait until dark, we might lose them.'

'Junior, shut up,' Curly said casually.

Junior whirled to face Curly, his hand moving to the butt of his revolver.

Clay moved between them. 'We've got work to do. Save this for later.'

After both men nodded, Clay turned to face the cowhands. Much as he disliked admitting it, Junior was right. They were running out of time. A canyon a few miles south of them led to the gold district, and if Clay's theory was correct, the rustlers were not far from their destination.

'I'll do some scouting,' Clay said. 'Wait here.'

'Clay,' Wash said, 'some of us had better go with you–'

'This is my job,' Clay said. He moved to his horse and swung up into the saddle.

Riding out of the trees, Clay made a beeline for the hills. He had never felt so vulnerable, or so foolish. In the quarter of an hour it took to reach the cover of the hills, Clay expected at any moment to hear the crack of a rifle shot, and perhaps catch a glimpse of smoke as he had that cold day when he'd been bushwacked.

But he reached the slope of a hill without anyone firing at him. He dismounted. Leaving the gelding behind, Clay climbed the hill and dropped to his knees near the top.

Beyond this hill was a series of lower ones. Looking in all directions, Clay still saw no tracks or signs of movement, no dust in the air churned by driven cattle.

Clay turned and plunged back down the slope to his horse. He jumped into the saddle and rode upslope, angling northward to the top of the hill. The rustlers were somewhere behind them, Clay decided. He rode over one low hill after another, rising up in the stirrups as he approached each crest, peering intently ahead.

His gelding gave the first warning. The horse tossed his head and whickered. Clay reined the animal around, looking for the nearest cover. A narrow draw between this hill and the one behind him led straight to a high, rocky ridge.

Clay rode down into the draw, turning upslope when he reached the bottom. Spurring his horse to a fast trot, Clay rode toward the ridge that rose up less than a quarter of a mile away.

Near the end of the draw Clay reined up. The way was blocked by a pile of boulders higher than a barn. Sliding out of the saddle, Clay led the gelding through a narrow passage around the pile of boulders. Behind was a growth of tall brush.

Tying his horse to the brush, Clay climbed out of the draw to the base of the ridge. There he saw a fissure, a jagged opening in the stone ridge that led up to a ledge. Glancing up, and all around, Clay made a quick decision.

Moving to the fissure, Clay braced himself with one foot and grasped the edge of the opening with his hands.

He raised his other foot, found a hold, and climbed up as far as his leg would stretch. He grabbed a higher handhold, then raised his other foot until he found another hold.

In a few minutes of climbing in this way, Clay reached the ledge above. He lay flat on his stomach, breathing hard. Looking out over the grassy plains, he saw the cotton-wood grove where the cowhands waited far to the south. The hills stretched out beneath his gaze, and when he looked back to the north, he saw a haze of dust rising into the air.

A few minutes later cattle drifted into his panoramic view. Two riders flanked the herd, and two more brought up the rear. When the animals drew closer, Clay saw Circle R brands on the cattle. The riders passed, slowly pushing the herd over one hill after another.

Their progress would have been faster out

on the grassy plain, but the hills gave the rustlers cover, and Clay could tell that the drovers felt secure. They sat their saddles easily, whistling or calling to the cattle in order to keep them bunched. Had he not known better, he would have thought these men were ordinary cowhands moving a herd to a new pasture.

When the herd had passed, Clay noticed two more riders coming. They were far enough back to escape the dust raised by the cattle.

Each led a pack animal, and they rode at a slow pace, looking back over their shoulders every time they topped a hill. Clay saw that they were heavily armed. Both wore two revolvers and carried rifles in saddle boots. One, wearing a tan hat, had a pair of field glasses on a strap around his neck.

Soon they drew even with him, and reined up. Breathless, Clay watched as they turned their horses and rode straight toward him, moving along the crest of the hill above the draw where he'd left his horse.

Less than fifty yards away from the rock ledge, the two rustlers halted and dismounted. Clay could hear their voices as they talked with their backs to him. One was squat and red-haired and dressed like a cowhand. The other, the man with the tan hat, wore khaki trousers and a brown shirt.

As Clay watched, this man raised the field

glasses to his eyes and surveyed the terrain all around except for the rock ledge behind him. One of the pack animals moved, and turned his side toward Clay. The brand on his flank was H-T.

Clay thought quickly. At any moment his gelding might whicker. If they discovered a saddled horse with a Circle R brand, the rustlers would realize they were being watched and would soon discover Clay.

He had nowhere to go. As he drew his revolver, Clay felt certain that these men were not only the murderers of Bill and Zeb, but were the rustlers who had raided the north pasture the year before. And one of them might be the man who had ambushed him.

Still, he could not bring himself to shoot them down with no warning, or no chance to surrender.

The smell of cigarette smoke drifted up to him. While the man in the tan hat systematically surveyed their back trail through his field glasses, the second man had rolled a smoke and lit it. In the next moment Clay's horse whinnied.

CHAPTER 19

The rustlers did not react immediately, probably at first thinking the whinny had come from one of their own mounts. But then the truth dawned on them.

As Clay watched, the rustlers slowly looked at one another, then spun around, drawing their handguns.

Looking in all directions except upward, where Clay was hiding, they advanced toward the rock wall. The moment the man wearing the tan hat caught sight of Clay's gelding, he stopped and aimed his revolver down into the draw. The red-haired rustler did the same.

Clay sat up, taking deliberate aim with his Colt .45. 'One more move, and you're dead.'

Startled, the two rustlers stared up at the rock ledge a dozen feet over their heads, and for a long moment there was a deadly silence as they saw Clay. The pair did not lower their guns, and Clay held his revolver, steadily aiming at the man wearing the tan hat.

It was he who broke the silence. 'You'll never get both of us,' he said.

Clay had spotted him as the leader of the

pair. 'You'll be the first to die. You ready?'

The tan-hatted rustler hesitated, and his partner cast a glance at him.

Clay suddenly lowered his Colt a few inches and squeezed the trigger, firing a shot that sprayed dirt and stones at their feet. Both men leaped backward.

Cocking the Colt .45, Clay again took aim at the rustler wearing the tan hat.

'Now, hold on—' the man said.

'No more talk,' Clay said. 'Drop those guns, or you're dead.'

The tan-hatted rustler's jaw tightened as he stared at Clay.

'Now!' Clay ordered.

After a moment, both men reluctantly dropped their handguns.

'Take two steps back,' Clay said, 'and lie down.'

'What?' the short, red-haired rustler asked, squinting up at Clay.

'You heard me,' Clay said. 'Move back away from those guns and lie down on the ground.'

The red-haired man did so immediately, and the rustler wearing the tan hat slowly backed up two paces. He dropped to his knees and stretched out on the ground, never taking his eyes from Clay.

With his Colt .45 trained on the prone rustlers, Clay started to climb down the ledge. Grasping the ledge with his free hand, he half turned and lowered one leg over the side, probing for a foothold with the toe of his boot.

Finding a foothold, Clay braced his weight on the one foot and lowered himself, catching a second foothold with his other boot. Both rustlers watched intently, waiting for him to make a mistake.

Keeping his gun steadily on them, Clay gripped the stone edge with his free hand, feeling sharp rock cut into his palm, his fingers pressing into the rough surface. Sweat rolled from his brow.

Another step down, and Clay let loose with his free hand suddenly, turned in the air as he jumped, and landed in a crouch, facing the two rustlers.

'You've got sand, mister,' the rustler in the tan hat said. 'You ain't home free yet, though, not by a long shot.'

The man was right. In shooting, Clay had taken the risk that his shot had been heard by the other rustlers. But he'd shown that he would use his gun, and it had given him the upper hand.

Clay kicked the rustlers' guns away, then ordered the red-haired rustler to go down into the draw and get his gelding. The other rustler gave his partner a hard look.

'Don't grease our skids,' he said.

Clay aimed his gun at the red-haired rustler's knee. 'I'm in a hurry. Do as I say, and we'll all ride out of here in one piece. If I have to leave you, I'll maim you.'

The bluff worked. The red-haired rustler got to his feet and went down the slope. Clay watched him untie the gelding and lead the animal back up.

Taking the reins of his own horse in hand, Clay mounted. His gun held ready, he guided his gelding to the rustlers' mounts. Taking their rifles out of the saddle boots, he tossed the guns down into the draw. Then he loosened a rope from one of the saddles and brought it back to the red-haired man.

'Tie your partner's hands behind his back,' Clay said, 'and help him up on his horse.'

The rustler wearing the tan hat slowly rose to his feet, staring angrily at his partner.

'Well, what do you expect me to do?' the red-haired rustler demanded in a loud whisper. Without waiting for a reply, he moved behind the tan-hatted man and tied his hands. Then he helped him up on his horse.

'All right,' Clay said. 'Now you mount up and take the lead rope of those pack animals.'

Clay then pointed toward the grassland beyond with his revolver. 'Ride straight out there. Fast.' He added, 'Break out of a straight line, and I'll shoot.'

Following the pair down the slope toward the flat grassland, Clay kept a wary eye to the south. No riders appeared from that direction. Either the other four rustlers had not heard the shot from his revolver, or they had attached no significance to the firing of a single shot.

Out on the grassland Clay ordered the red-haired rustler to turn southward and ride to the grove of cottonwood trees on the horizon.

When they were a quarter of a mile away from the grove. Clay saw riders coming. The cowhands soon arrived on their galloping horses. All the men were brandishing guns.

'We was just about to come looking for you,' Curly said, as the cowhands gathered around Clay and the two rustlers. 'You was gone too long.'

'I got myself in a little bind,' Clay said. He motioned to his prisoners. 'This pair was riding rear guard for the rustlers with the herd.'

'We didn't have nothing to do with that herd,' the man wearing the tan hat said, looking angrily from Clay to the cowhands.

Clay said to him, 'There isn't a man here who wouldn't like to string you both up and leave you hanging. You might want to keep your mouth shut, and hope we take you in peaceably.'

Clay turned to Specs. 'You and Hank run this pair back into the trees and tie them up. We'll come back for you.'

Specs nodded.

'Four rustlers are riding with the herd,' Clay said to the others. 'With a show of force, I think we can take them. Any of you who want out of this party, say so now.'

The men were silent until Junior shouted, 'Let's get after them!' He waved his revolver in the air.

'Put that thing away, kid,' Clay said. He looked at all the cowhands. 'All right, let's ride.'

CHAPTER 20

Clay led the cowhands across the grassland toward the hills. He cut an angle to the south, trying to estimate how far the herd had been driven since he'd last seen it.

A quarter of an hour later he caught sight of dust in the air over the low hills. He spurred his gelding to a high lope, quickly gaining ground on the unseen cattle.

At the base of a wide draw between two hills, Clay signaled the men to halt. He reined his horse down and turned to face them.

Quickly counting off half the men, Clay said, 'Curly, take your crew up this draw and ride in behind the herd. The rest of you come with me. We'll grab the flankers and

170

try to take control of the herd.'

Clay added, 'If there's going to be any shooting, let the rustlers start it – then give them hell.'

Clay touched spurs to his gelding, turned the horse around, and rode off with half of the group following. Junior was among them, and his little mare leaped forward as the kid dug his heels into her sides.

Clay rode hard for two hundred yards, then looked at his right, up another draw, and saw cattle. He slowed his horse and led the way there, drawing his revolver. Glancing back to see the others do the same, he caught a glimpse of Junior's expectant face under the brim of his hat. The big Remington revolver was in his hand now.

In the next moment, looking straight ahead, Clay saw one of the flanking drovers. The man rode down into the draw beside the herd, casting an unconcerned glance at Clay and the men bunched behind him. Then the man's mouth and eyes stretched open in amazement.

Clay sharply spurred his horse, aiming his Colt .45 at the surprised drover. The man reined his horse to a halt in the bottom of the draw and raised his free hand over his head.

'That's the smartest thing you've done all week,' Clay said, halting his horse beside the man. He reached over to the drover's waist and lifted the revolver from his holster.

Clay tossed the gun back to John Leed. 'Take this man back to the cottonwood grove.'

After Leed escorted the drover away, Clay said, 'You men ride to the rear of the herd and help the others pick up the two who are riding drag. I'll cut in front of the herd and get the other flanker—'

A burst of shots interrupted him, and Clay gave the cowhands an urgent signal to ride back.

'I'll get that other flanker, Clay!' Junior shouted, and his horse leaped away.

Too late to call after him, Clay turned his horse and saw Junior ride with the herd, quickly overtaking the cattle. The steers were starting to mill, and several in the middle of the herd had thrown their heads up, looking for a place to run.

Over the brown, moving mass, through the haze of dust churned by the cattle, Clay saw the other drover. Wearing a handkerchief over his mouth and nose against the dust, the man was looking over his shoulder, obviously wondering about the shooting.

Clay rode after Junior, letting his gelding run as hard as the animal could. The cattle were spooked now, and critters spilled out in front of him, bawling and rolling their eyes in fear.

His horse suddenly shied as the horns of a

running steer slashed his ribs. Clay let the gelding take a wider berth, galloping over the hill and down into the next shallow draw, and up the far side of the next hill. Behind, more shots were fired, and the drumming of hooves grew louder and louder, like a deadly crescendo.

Clay lost his Stetson as the gelding became caught up in the spirit of the race, galloping recklessly over one low hill after another, plunging ahead of the stampeding steers.

The cattle had spread out like grain spilled on the ground, but in the next hundred yards Clay overtook them and rode around the lead animals. He angled toward the steeper hills that shouldered against the Bear Paws, and the running steers swept past him, smashing everything in their path.

On a hilltop, Clay reined up, letting his heaving horse rest. From here he had a commanding view of the rolling ground the herd had just come over. He saw no sign of Junior.

Walking his horse down into the draw moments later, Clay heard a shot. Heading in the direction from which it came, he rode over several more hills, then turned up a draw. He saw the tracks of shod horses leading up toward the mountains.

The draw curved, and rounding the bend,

Clay saw the rump of a black horse ahead. He drew his gun and slowly rode ahead, noticing first the Circle R brand on the horse and then that it was the black mare ridden by Junior.

Junior was still in the saddle, whirling around when he suddenly became aware of Clay. For an instant they aimed their guns at one another.

Clay did not lower his Colt .45 until Junior returned his gun to his holster. Then Clay holstered his gun and rode ahead, pulling up beside the kid.

A dozen yards away this draw ended at a rock wall similar to the one Clay had climbed. Backed against the wall of stone was a horse, and at his feet lay the body of the rustler with the handkerchief over his mouth and nose. Through the man's chest was a black hole, ringed with blood.

'I ran him down,' Junior said, 'and the bastard went for his gun.'

Clay looked at the kid.

'I had to kill him, Clay,' Junior said. 'The bastard didn't give me any choice.'

Looking around at the ground, Clay asked, 'Where is his gun? His holster is empty.'

When Junior made no reply, Clay said, 'Looks to me like this man lost his handgun somewhere, maybe during the stampede.'

'I'm telling you the truth, Clay…' Junior's voice trailed off as he stared at the dead man. 'Happened fast ... I saw him go for his gun...'

Clay dismounted. 'Help me load him on his horse.'

Junior swung a leg over his saddle and dropped to the ground. 'Honest, Clay–'

'We'll talk about it later,' Clay interrupted. He knelt beside the dead man and pulled the dusty handkerchief off his face. Peaceful in repose, the man's eyes were closed, mouth slightly open. Clay had never seen him before.

'Grab on,' Clay said. He grasped the man's shoulders while Junior lifted under the knees. They carried the body to the horse and slung it over the saddle. Clay used the man's rope to secure him in the saddle.

Taking the reins of the horse, Clay mounted his gelding. He was aware that Junior stared after him as he rode out of the draw, but he did not return the kid's gaze.

On top of a nearby hill Clay saw the cowhands gathered around the two captured rustlers. The rustlers sat their horses, heads bowed. They looked up when Clay approached. The cowhands turned in their saddles, staring at the corpse.

'What happened?' Curly asked.

Clay made no reply, but he looked back at Junior.

Junior reined up a short distance away. 'I rode this one down, and the bastard went for his gun.' The kid added, 'It was him or me.'

A long silence followed. Clay broke it by asking Curly, 'Are any of our boys hurt?'

'Jack Grayson got winged,' Curly replied. 'Nothing too bad. He rode back to the grove on his own.'

Wash said, 'They gave up the fight soon as they figured out what they were up against.'

Clay nodded. To Curly and Wash, he said, 'We'll take this pair back to the cottonwood grove.'

Clay turned to the others. 'Ride after the herd and round up as many critters as you can before nightfall. Bring them to grove, and we'll finish the job in the morning.' He added, 'You did a good job of work here.'

CHAPTER 21

In Yellow Pine, Clay rode down the street to the telegraph office, feeling as if he'd been in the saddle a month. Behind him came Curly, Wash, and Junior. They rode guard over the five rustlers. The sixth had been buried near the cottonwood grove.

Under Specs's supervision, Clay had ordered the rest of the Circle R crew to drive the cattle back to the north pasture.

Clay reined up at the tie rail. He swung a leg over the saddle and slid to the ground. Climbing onto the platform, he was met in the doorway of the telegraph office by Henry Reid. A questioning look was on the telegrapher's face.

Before Reid could get his questions out, Clay asked, 'The county sheriff ever answer that wire a Circle R man sent the other day?'

Reid nodded, looking from Clay to the rustlers, and back again. 'Sheriff Barnes and a deputy came on yesterday's train. They rode out to the ranch. Didn't you see them?'

Clay shook his head tiredly. 'Haven't been home for a few days.'

'Looks like you've had trouble,' Reid said.

'Some,' Clay said, reaching to his bare head where his hat was supposed to be. He'd not had time to search for his Stetson after it had blown off his head when his horse galloped around the stampeding herd. Probably wasn't much left of it, anyway, he thought.

Clay sent Curly to the home ranch for the sheriff, then he, Wash, and Junior helped the bound rustlers out of their saddles and sat them in a row along the platform. All the while Reid asked questions, and learned from Junior how the rustlers had been captured.

Clay moved behind the rustlers and

slumped down on the platform, leaning back against the clapboard wall of the telegraph office.

Reid came to Clay and knelt beside him. 'Why do you do it?'

'Do what?' Clay asked, closing his eyes.

'Ride after a bunch of hardcases,' Reid said. 'That's a lawman's job.'

'If I'd waited for the law,' Clay said, 'Circle R stock would have been butchered, hides buried, and steaks on miners' plates.'

'Risking your neck for a mean old rancher,' Reid said. 'That's what I can't figure out.'

Clay opened his eyes and looked at the telegrapher.

'You not only run his ranch for him,' Reid went on, 'but you fight his battles. Why?'

Clay saw that he was genuinely mystified. 'My job is to hold the ranch together. I do it as best I can.'

'Risking your neck for damned little gain,' Reid said, shaking his head. 'A man as smart as you.'

Clay looked over the heads of the rustlers in front of him, past the horses and down the rutted street of Yellow Pine. Beyond were the vast grasslands, stretching to the far horizon.

Reid said in a low voice, 'I tried to do you a favor, Clay, by giving you a chance to buy into this town. You could have made your fortune, or close to it. But you just couldn't see it.'

Clay turned his gaze to the telegrapher. 'Two men can look at the same thing, Henry, and see something different.'

Clay got to his feet and walked down the street to Mays's General Store. He went inside and bought a new hat.

The county sheriff and his deputy arrived from the ranch late in the afternoon. From descriptions of the gang of rustlers the sheriff had, and their possession of two H-T pack animals, it was apparent the Circle R cowhands had captured the gang that had raided herds throughout northern Montana.

Junior gave a statement to the sheriff about the killing of the sixth rustler. Clay was not asked, and did not volunteer his belief that the rustler was unarmed when Junior shot him down. In the evening the lawmen stopped the westbound Great Northern. They loaded the horses and two pack animals in a stock car, then boarded with their prisoners.

Before climbing onto the coach, the sheriff reminded Clay that a court date in Great Falls would be set, and the Circle R men would have to appear for a hearing. Based on evidence and testimony given at this hearing, the district court judge would rule whether or not the accused rustlers would be bound over for trial.

Clay and Wash and Junior returned to the

home ranch, arriving long after dark. The Old Man had gone to bed, but when Clay walked to the ranch house from the barn he saw a light in Annie's room. He went into the kitchen for a lukewarm cup of coffee from the pot left on the stove. While he poured the thick brew, his eye was caught by a movement in the doorway to the main room of the house.

Clay turned and saw Annie come through the door. Her hair tumbled in soft curls to her shoulders. She wore a flannel robe. It was pulled snugly about her, emphasizing a slender waist and the full curve of her hips.

Without a word, she came across the kitchen to him, her eyes blinking rapidly. She threw her arms around him and pressed her head against his chest.

Clay held her tightly, hearing her cry softly. He caught the fresh scent of her hair, and was embarrassed. Trying to pull away, he said, 'I smell worse than my horse.'

After a moment, Annie loosened her hold and looked up at him. One cheek that had not been pressed against his shirt was wet with tears.

'I was afraid,' she said softly. 'Afraid you wouldn't come back.'

Clay felt drawn by her eyes, and he bent down and kissed her lightly and briefly.

'Tell me everything that happened,' she said, taking a step back and grasping his hands. 'Jess and I heard as much as Curly wanted to tell us, but I want to hear it from you.'

They sat at the mess table while Clay drank coffee laced with rye whiskey. He told Annie of the burial by moonlight of the two cowhands, and of the pursuit and capture of the rustlers.

Clay left out a few details, and one suspicion lurking in the back of his mind. He could not rid himself of the belief that Junior had murdered that fleeing rustler.

CHAPTER 22

Five days after the capture of the rustlers, Clay received word from a passing rider that a message awaited him at the telegraph office. The next day was Saturday, and at sundown he rode into Yellow Pine with the cowhands.

The men were bathed, shaved, and clothed in clean shirts and trousers, ready to let the tiger loose. Clay had told them that every drink between then and midnight would be paid for by the Circle R.

The message came from the clerk of district court in Great Falls. A hearing for the 'accused rustlers' was scheduled for the following week, and testimony would be required from all the cowhands who had taken part in the capture of the rustlers.

In addition, 'Junior Smith' would have to appear and give a statement regarding the killing of the sixth rustler. This statement had to be delivered in person to the judge, and would be entered into court records.

Clay folded the message and jammed it into the pocket of his trousers. Leaving a 30,000-acre cattle ranch at roundup time with no cowhands was impossible. How could a Montana judge make such a fool request?

Clay penciled out a terse reply, stating that he would be present for the hearing, with as many cowhands as he could spare. In truth, he planned to take two or three men with him, along with Junior.

Henry Reid tapped out Clay's message, then leaned back in his swivel chair and looked up at Clay. 'I know what you've been hearing lately.'

Not understanding what the telegrapher meant, Clay looked at him questioningly.

Reid gestured toward the empty street outside as though that answered all questions.

Clay turned and looked out the small window in the door, then turned his gaze back to the small, pale-complexioned man before him. 'You're still a believer in Yellow Pine's future?'

'Damned right, I am,' Reid said, coming down into his chair. 'The townsite's all laid out, just waiting for folks. This time next year new buildings will line main street, and out there where there's nothing but grass, you'll see houses on new streets.' He added, 'And nobody'll be saying Henry Reid's a fool.'

Clay did not understand that parting remark until he walked into the Bon Ton a few minutes later. From Frenchy he heard a different account of Yellow Pine's future.

'Al Mays sold his town lots,' the saloon-keeper said, stroking his pointed beard. 'The boom is over. Even the railroad men say so. Al makes no secret of it. He and Henry have had a falling out. His fifty percent loss has made him an unhappy man.'

'That could spoil a man's naturally good humor,' Clay allowed.

'His dreams were soap bubbles,' Frenchy said. 'Shiny and filled with rainbows for a short time – dried up now.'

Clay grinned at Frenchy's fancy talk. 'Henry Reid isn't giving up his dream of being a town builder.'

Frenchy nodded, making a sad expression.

'What about your dreams?' Clay asked.

'So?' Frenchy said with a shrug. 'My fortune comes more slowly. Nothing changes. I have time.' He glanced down the length of the bar at the cowhands lined up elbow to elbow, mugs of foaming beer in front of them.

'Drink up,' Frenchy said, smiling. 'Drink up.'

Clay also learned from the saloonkeeper that news from the gold district was not good for would-be town founders. It was becoming apparent that Majestic Mining & Milling effectively controlled the large vein of gold that set off the rush last spring. Since then, no other gold-bearing outcroppings had been discovered.

Majestic settled into the work of mining gold and shipping ore. The construction crew bossed by Angus Macdougal had built a boarding house and a company store. The store was stocked with supplies brought in on the rail spur.

Drawing their pay of $3.50 a day, the miners slept in a company bed and ate company food. What remained of their salaries was spent in the nearby tent town that had moved lock, stock, and crib from Yellow Pine to the end of the rail spur.

By the end of August, autumn was coming to the high country, and with the chilly night breezes came a scent of winter. The prospectors who had not hired on with Majestic packed up and left, empty-handed. In September most of the hangers-on went after them, the tent gamblers, saloonkeepers, and prostitutes, all heading for a new mining camp in the Colorado Rockies. This one was rumored, as were all new gold strikes, to be the richest one of all.

Clay left the Bon Ton early, riding out of Yellow Pine before dark. On the edge of town were trampled weeds where not long ago a network of boardwalks had connected dozens of tents, shacks, and the cribs of Four-bit Flats.

Clay's gelding splashed across Cottonwood Creek. In the evening light the railroader's lamp glowed red beside the door of Dirty Gertie's cabin. She's outlasted the competition, Clay thought as he rode past. He urged his horse across the grasslands toward the home ranch. His thoughts were on Annie.

He was uncertain whether Annie had changed so much in the last ten months, or if his perception of her had changed. Some of both, he guessed, recalling that day when she'd climbed out of Rawls's buggy and looked uncertainly around at the log ranch buildings and the long stretch of the grassy valley.

She might have looked like a girl then, but she was a woman now, and the mother of a growing baby. Annie worked from sunup to sundown and sometimes later, whether she was caring for her child or the Old Man, washing clothes or working beside Cookie in the kitchen.

185

Cookie was not so young himself, and Clay knew that without Annie's help that old cowhand turned cook might not have made it through the summer. Between cooking for more cowhands than had ever worked on the Circle R to feeding a haying crew for two weeks, the kitchen work was just about overwhelming. But everyday at mealtimes Annie was at Cookie's side while the Old Man sat in the other room carrying on long monologues with the baby.

First there had been little inclination for romance, Clay reflected, then there had been no time. But his few moments with Annie had left deepening impressions and vivid memories. The time when she had been manhandled by the one-eyed prospector, Clay had nearly gone out of his mind with rage.

At that moment, more than any previous time, he understood the depth of his feelings toward her. She must have sensed the change, too, and shared the bond. Afterward, she cast long looks at him, holding him with her gaze, and then the night he'd returned after delivering the rustlers to the county sheriff, she had pressed her body against him, clinging and sobbing with relief that he'd come back unhurt.

Every week Cookie brought back mail to the home ranch along with weekly supplies from Al Mays's store. Clay was aware that

Annie received many letters from her family in Baltimore. And from her distant mood after reading one of these, Clay wondered if she was being pressured to return.

By the fading light of evening Clay dimly saw the haystacks in the fields. Ahead in the long valley were the squat ranch buildings of the Circle R. Rectangles of light shone from the windows, and beckoned Clay. Over this darkening land arched the pale sky, now showing stars.

This peaceful scene, the sight and scent of the landscape, brought a new and urgent thought to Clay's mind. Annie might leave.

CHAPTER 23

The ranch was Saturday-night quiet. Specs and another cowhand, along with Junior, were in the bunkhouse. As Clay crossed the yard from the horse barn, he saw Cookie through the open doorway of the cabin. Booted feet propped up on his bunk, the old-timer read a tattered copy of the *Police Gazette* by lamplight, ignoring the moths that darted about.

Entering the kitchen through the side door, Clay saw a glow of light from the main room. He went into the room and saw a single lamp burning, but no one was there.

The door to the Old Man's bedroom was closed, and as Clay moved in front of the fireplace he saw that Annie's door stood half open. He hesitated, then moved to it, drawn by the soft sounds of her voice.

'Annie,' Clay said.

'Clay?'

'Yeah.'

She pulled the door open. 'Come in. I'm just putting William to bed.'

Clay stepped into the room, returning Annie's quick smile. The baby lay in a wicker cradle, looking intently at his mother, cooing.

Annie's smile faded as she took a second, longer look at Clay. 'Is something wrong?'

Clay managed a lopsided grin. 'Nope.'

'You seem so serious,' she said, smiling again. Turning to the cradle, she finished tucking a blanket around her baby.

'I see you pried him away from Jess tonight,' Clay said.

Annie laughed softly. 'Sometimes even Jess gets tired of this perpetual-motion machine. Tonight after supper he went straight to bed, and I haven't seen him since.'

She straightened up and looked at Clay. In the moment of silence that followed, he searched for words but found none. Then the baby cooed again.

Clay said, 'I've been wanting to talk to

you, Annie.'

She nodded and whispered, 'If we leave the room, he'll go to sleep.' She added, 'I hope.'

Clay moved to the door and stepped into the main room. Annie blew out the lamp in her bedroom and came out. Pausing at the door, she looked back into the darkened room.

'Sometimes he protests,' she said over her shoulder.

Clay said, 'If we go out on the porch, you'll be able to hear him, won't you?'

'I sure will,' Annie said. 'When William wants to make himself heard, he can wake up everyone on this ranch.'

No moon was in the sky, but the land was faintly lighted by stars. Clay sat beside Annie on the step of the porch, and looked up. Pinpoints of white light were sprinkled across the black sky.

'I've been thinking,' Clay said, turning to Annie. His throat tightened. 'I've – I've been thinking about a talk we had last winter?' He added, 'About the future.'

'I remember,' Annie said.

'Well, I don't know a whole lot more now than I did then,' Clay said. 'Except for one thing.' He looked at her by the golden glow of lamplight coming through the open doorway of the ranch house. Far away a coyote yipped, and was answered by another.

Clay lifted his hand to the side of her face. The soft warmth of her flesh stirred him, and thickened his voice. 'I love you, Annie.'

'Oh, Clay,' she whispered.

'I don't think of the future anymore,' he said, 'without thinking of you.'

He lowered his hand, and she clasped both of her hands around it. 'I know you've got a lot to think about,' Clay said. 'Not only your future, but your baby's future. I don't have much to offer you, and you'd probably have an easier life if you went back East–'

'Clay, stop it,' Annie said. She squeezed his hand. 'I won't go back there. I've made up my mind. I'll stay here, and I'm going to keep my baby.' She leaned against him. 'I love you, Clay. I have since the first day I saw you.'

Clay was amazed at this remark.

'And don't tell me you have nothing to offer,' she said. 'We have the future, and we'll build a life together.'

'That's what I want,' Clay said. He leaned down and kissed her, feeling his own lips tremble for a moment. Then he put his arms around her, and their embrace was long and hard.

CHAPTER 24

On Sunday afternoon Clay brought Specs, two cowhands, and Junior into the ranch house where they stood before the Old Man.

'We have to appear in court in Great Falls,' Clay said, pulling the telegraphed message out of his hip pocket. He handed it to Rawls.

'A hearing is being held for those rustlers,' Clay went on, 'and we'll give testimony. Junior has to appear, too, and give a statement about the killing of–'

'Hell, I already gave my statement,' Junior said. 'I told the sheriff what happened.'

'The judge has to hear it, too,' Clay said.

Junior turned away, swearing.

'How long will you be gone, Clay?' Rawls asked, looking up from the telegraphed message.

'A couple of days,' Clay said, 'maybe three. I want Specs to ramrod while I'm gone. You can adjust his pay for that, can't you, Jess?'

Rawls nodded.

'All right with you, Specs?' Clay asked, turning to the lanky cowhand.

'I reckon so,' Specs drawled. He thought a

moment, and asked, 'We'll be gathering stock for roundup, won't we?'

Clay nodded. 'I want those hills up north scoured. I think we're short. No telling how many head were scattered through that country when the rustlers hit.'

'We'll do a proper job of it, Clay,' Specs said.

Junior slapped his hands together in frustration and anger. 'Damn, why the hell should I have to go into court?'

'Like I said–' Clay began.

'What happens if I don't?' Junior snapped.

'The judge will issue a warrant for your arrest,' Clay said, 'and a lawman will come after you.'

Rawls said to the kid, 'There ain't nothing to it. Just tell the judge what happened like you told the county sheriff. Some clerk will write down your words, and that'll be the end of it.'

Clay regarded Junior. The kid stood still, arms stiffly held at his sides, head bowed.

Rawls went on. 'It'll look bad for you if you don't show up and give your statement.'

Junior turned abruptly and walked out of the room. Rawls called after him, but the kid left the ranch house, leaving the door standing open behind him.

Late that night, after the last lamp had been extinguished in the bunkhouse, Clay met Annie on the porch of the ranch house.

After a kiss and a long embrace, they sat together on the first step of the porch. Clay put his arm around her shoulders, and they looked out at the darkened land and the starry night sky.

'When are we going to tell people, Clay?' she whispered.

'After fall roundup,' Clay replied. 'Before that, I don't want these cowhands ribbing us and dreaming up practical jokes.' He added, 'Besides, after roundup I'll have some bonus money, and we can go on a honeymoon somewhere.'

Annie took his hand in both of hers and kissed it. 'Oh, Clay, I'm so excited. I want us to be married right now.'

'That's my feeling, too,' Clay said. 'But I think we'd better wait.'

'I know,' she said, pausing. 'It's exciting to have a secret like this. I feel like I'm walking on air.'

The talked about how they would live. The cabin could be fixed up for them, and Cookie could move into her room in the house. Plans came readily to Annie's mind, and she talked of them excitedly.

Clay didn't say so, but he was concerned about the way Rawls would react when he learned they planned to marry. Annie assumed he would be as thrilled as she was, but Clay had doubts. To him, this might mean Clay was taking Annie and the baby away from him.

Clay himself did not know what the immediate future held, and he did not raise the question with Annie. Time for that later, he reckoned. She was not looking past their marriage, and for now, Clay decided not to, either.

Next evening after supper Clay made a swing through the bunkhouse, making certain the two cowhands were ready to go in the morning, and he reminded the kid that they had a train to catch. Junior replied with a single nod of his head.

In the morning the kid was gone.

Clay discovered that Junior had taken the black mare and the saddle and bridle. From the kitchen the kid had stolen tins of food and several pounds of beef and elk jerky Cookie had laid away in the pantry. This theft was discovered just before early breakfast was served.

Clay heard the Old Man in the other room. He went in and found Rawls standing before his desk. It had been ransacked. The cash box was empty.

'That damned kid,' Rawls said after Clay told him of Junior's disappearance. 'I fed him and put clothes on his back, gave him work, and look what he done.'

Staring at the empty cash box, Rawls said, 'Take some of the boys and ride him down.'

'Jess, I'm leaving on the train for Great

Falls,' Clay said. 'I'm taking two cowhands with me–'

'What for?' Rawls demanded.

'To testify–'

'Oh, I recollect,' Rawls said, waving his hand impatiently at Clay. His face went slack, as though suddenly tired. 'Hell, we'll let the damned kid go. Good riddance.'

Upon his return from Great Falls, Clay went into the ranch house and reported to the Old Man. The judge had found cause to bind the five rustlers over for trial, and a court date had been set for the week after the Circle R was scheduled to ship cattle to Chicago.

Rawls nodded while he listened, but his mind was obviously on other matters. 'You'll have to make the trip alone this year, Clay. I'm too damned stove up for that train ride.'

'All right,' Clay said.

Rawls looked at him. 'You can handle it, can't you?'

Clay nodded. 'Yeah.' He asked, 'Any sign of Junior?'

'No,' Rawls said. 'He's long gone.'

'The judge in Great Falls issued a bench warrant for his arrest,' Clay said. 'He asked me to get a message off and let the county sheriff know if the kid had come back, or if he'd been seen around here.'

Rawls shook his head. 'He ain't coming back. Not this time.'

Clay agreed, but did not reveal why. In Great Falls he'd helped the sheriff write up a physical description of Junior that would be sent out to towns across Montana. Something in the description seemed familiar to the lawman, and he searched through a stack of 'Wanted' posters. He found the one he wanted.

Samuel Dillard was an 18-year-old from Chicago who was wanted for the murder of his father and the killings of two policemen who had tried to take him into custody. Dillard was last seen by trainmen in the Chicago rail yards. Clay noticed that date coincided with the time Junior first landed in Yellow Pine and went to work for Frenchy as a swamper.

After supper took Annie for a walk. He told her about his court appearance, and how the sheriff might have learned Junior's true identity. He did not mention that Samuel Dillard was described as 'extremely dangerous.'

Clay sprang a surprise on Annie when he drew a sheet of paper out of his pocket and handed it to her. The document was a marriage license.

'Oh, Clay,' Annie said, her eyes sparkling in delight. 'I love you!'

By the light of the rising sun in the morning Clay gave the cowhands their assignments. After the men topped off their horses and rode out, Clay saddled his gelding and went to Yellow Pine to send his message to the sheriff.

Crossing Cottonwood Creek, an idea came to him. He turned in midstream and rode back to Dirty Gertie's. When he reined up and stepped down from the saddle, the door opened and the big woman appeared.

Dressed in her long, shapeless gown, she looked steadily at Clay, but said nothing.

'Remember me?' Clay asked.

'Course I do,' she said. 'Circle R. You're the ramrod out there.'

'A while back Mr Rawls asked you to tell him if you should ever see his wrangler again,' Clay said. 'That thin young kid with dark hair—'

'I 'member,' she said, her small black eyes narrowing.

'Was he here four nights ago?' Clay asked.

Gertie shook her head.

'When was the last time you saw Junior?' Clay asked.

'I only seen him that once,' Gertie said, 'when you and Mr Rawls came hunting him.' She stared at Clay. 'I ain't lying. I wouldn't lie to you or Mr Rawls.'

Clay believed her. This had been a long shot, anyway, thinking Junior might have come here the night he had emptied out the Old Man's cashbox. If the kid had a brain in his head, he'd ridden hard and fast in a straight line away from the Circle R. He was out of the state by now, or if he'd ridden north he was out of the country.

CHAPTER 25

The gather of Circle R stock for fall roundup went smoothly. This year Clay was glad he'd hired a large crew. He'd been right in believing that more than a hundred head of cattle had been scattered into the hills beyond the north pasture. A rough tally was made as the herds were drifted south to winter pasture, and the total fit with Clay's estimation.

The four-year-old steers were cut from the herds and slowly driven down the long grassy valley toward the loading pens in Yellow Pine. By the time the Great Northern train brought stock cars to the siding, Clay would be ready to move cattle to the pens in an orderly procession.

For the cowhands, shipping cattle to the Chicago stockyards was more reward than work. Another profitable season on the Circle R meant the promise of smooth whiskey and smooth-legged women in the big city. That promise alone was sometimes enough to keep a man going when the work got tough or dangerous, or the weather got blistering hot or bitterly cold, or when feelings grew testy in the bunkhouse. In the back of a seasoned cowhand's mind was always the memory of stretching out on sheets in a real bed upstairs in Sally's Palace, and the boozy vision of a voluptuous woman coming across the room to the bedside, shedding her satin gown and bending down to stroke a sheer stocking from one leg and then the other, all with tantalizing slowness.

After the sale of cattle that fall, Clay rode in the passenger coach with the dozing, bruised cowhands. Wash reclined in the seat beside him, and across the aisle sat Curly, one eye nearly swollen shut. As always, Curly claimed to have won his fights with the Chicago saloon-men, but he'd never be able to prove it by his looks.

Rawls had not changed his mind about making the trip to Chicago, as Clay had suspected he would, and for the first time in more than a quarter of a century, the sale of Circle R stock had not been personally supervised by the man known in Union Stockyards as 'the pioneer rancher from Montana.'

Change. Clay thought of the changes he'd seen this year, and of his own life changes. If an era was ending when Rawls stayed home this fall, maybe another was beginning. Clay would soon become a family man.

Clay closed his eyes, resting his head against the back of the upholstered seat. He felt the steady vibration of the train as it rolled across empty countryside at twenty miles an hour. Not long ago marriage had been only a vague speculation in his private thoughts. Now it was an impending reality, and he found it difficult to imagine.

In Yellow Pine shortly after dawn, the cowhands climbed off the train and mounted saddle horses brought to town by Specs. The Old Man was not there. After the hands rode out for the ranch, Clay performed Rawls's ritual and paid off the Circle R bill at Mays's General Store & Post Office.

Clay then crossed the rutted street and deposited five thousand dollars in Frenchy's safe, cash that Rawls referred to as 'operating money.' Most of the money from the sale of cattle had been deposited in Rawls's account in a Chicago bank.

Those chores done, Clay swung up into the saddle and rode for home.

At the home ranch Clay could hardly keep his eyes off Annie as he met her and the Old Man in the main room of the ranch house. He handed Rawls the statement from his Chicago bank, along with Frenchy's receipt, and gave his report. It was a good one. More

Circle R cattle had been sold this year than ever before, and the highest price per pound of beef on the hoof had been paid.

'You've kept this outfit in the profit column ever' year you've ramrodded,' Rawls said, looking up at Clay from his favorite chair. 'And this year you done my work for me. I'm obliged, Clay.'

Rawls reached into his vest pocket and pulled out a slip of paper. He thrust it out to Clay. 'This here's for you.'

Clay took the folded slip of paper and opened it, seeing a check made out to him. The amount penned in a shaky hand was one thousand dollars.

'Jess–' Clay began.

Rawls held up his hand. 'No arguin' now. That money's yours. It's been a hell of a year, and you earned ever' penny.'

Clay looked at Annie. She smiled and moved closer to him. Clay put his arm around her, and turned to see a quizzical look on the Old Man's face.

'There's something we've been wanting to talk to you about, Jess,' Clay said with a lopsided grin.

'Well, I'll be damned,' Rawls muttered.

Annie laughed warmly. She left Clay's side and knelt before Rawls, taking his hand.

'We're getting married,' Clay said, 'as soon as we can pack up and find a judge.'

'Pack up,' Rawls repeated.

'For our honeymoon,' Annie said.

'Oh,' Rawls said quietly. 'You're coming back.'

'Of course we are, Jess,' Annie said. 'This is our home.'

'Yeah, but for how long?' he asked, glancing up at Clay. Rawls quickly added, 'Hell, it ain't none of my business. I reckon you know my feelings.'

'We do, Jess,' Clay said.

The Old Man looked fondly at Annie. 'That boy of yours is gong to have a real man for a father.'

'I know, Jess,' Annie murmured. Rising, she put her arms around his neck and hugged him.

Rawls got out of his chair, extending his hand to Clay. 'Take good care of her.'

'I will,' Clay said, shaking the Old Man's gnarled hand. He held up the check and said, 'This makes a fine wedding present, Jess.'

Rawls shook his head. 'That's wages, Clay. You risked your life for that money.' He turned abruptly and walked away, entering the bedroom. He pulled the door shut.

Clay reached out and took Annie's hand.

'Is he unhappy?' she whispered.

'I don't know,' Clay said. 'I think he's surprised, mostly.'

'I don't want our happiness to make him unhappy,' Annie said.

In the morning Clay gave the cowhands their assignments and watched them ride out. He worked in the horse barn for a while, then saddled his gelding. But as he left the ranch, he saw a single rider coming up the valley. The man was riding hard.

Clay turned and rode out to meet him, sensing urgency in his manner. When the rider drew closer, Clay recognized him as a cowhand who worked for the DHS.

'Clay!' he shouted, waving his free hand over his head. The DHS horse was lathered, and when the cowhand came near, the tired animal slowed to a walk.

'It's Frenchy,' the cowhand said breathlessly. 'Murdered.'

Clay stared at him.

The cowhand was narrow-faced, and now his expression was intense. He swallowed and caught his breath.

'Frenchy was beaten to death during the night,' the cowhand said. 'His safe was cleaned out.'

Clay shook his head in disbelief, unable to speak.

'I'll carry the news to the Lazy T,' the cowhand said. 'Can you loan me a horse?'

Nodding, Clay looked back at the corral adjoining the horse barn. 'Take that big bay out of the corral. He'll run all day.' He turned his head back to the cowhand, and they exchanged a long look.

'Awfulest thing I ever saw,' the cowhand said.

Clay tried to gather his thoughts. 'Was the safe blown open?'

The cowhand thought a moment, then shook his head. 'No, it wasn't. The doors are standing open, like the safe was opened by combination.' He asked, 'Does it make a difference how it was opened?'

'Might,' Clay said. 'If the safe was blown, I'd think some miner or prospector was involved. But since it was opened by combination the night after Circle R money was put in there, that's something else.'

CHAPTER 26

Bright morning sunlight streamed over the false front of the Bon Ton Saloon. The front door stood open. Clay tied his horse at the rail and went in. He saw the blanket-covered corpse on the dirt floor near the brass foot rail of the bar.

Clay walked through the empty saloon to the body. He knelt and lifted a corner of the blanket. By the light from the open door he saw the ruined face of Frenchy, pale with dark bruises, and unmoving.

'I found him like that, Clay.'

Startled, Clay shot a glance over his shoulder and saw Al Mays step through the doorway.

The storekeeper crossed the room, talking all the way. 'When I got up this morning, I happened to look over here and saw the door standing open... Knew right away something was wrong, bad wrong. Ever get a feeling like that? Runs a chill straight to your toes.'

Clay stood up, facing the storekeeper. His full beard and mustache gave him a forlorn appearance. Clay sensed that he wanted to talk.

'You hear or see anyone around here last night, Al?' Clay asked.

'No,' Mays said with finality. 'Nobody did. I asked around. Nobody even heard a horse during the night.'

Turning away, Clay walked to the saloon's back room. Beside Frenchy's bunk stood the tall steel safe. The thick double doors were ajar. On the smooth, nickle-plated handle of one was a smear of blood, dark now.

Clay pulled the doors open. Except for some papers and leather-bound ledger books, the shelves were empty.

Al Mays moved into the doorway behind Clay. 'Someone did a quiet job of robbing this safe and beating Frenchy to death. Beat him with some heavy, like a hammer or something.'

Clay nodded, but he believed Mays had it backward. Blood on the handle of the safe door meant that Frenchy had been killed first, then the safe had been opened. The doors had not been forced, Clay saw, when he looked for deep scratches in the thick steel plate.

'You didn't find the weapon?' Clay asked.

'No,' Mays said. He paused. 'A DHS cow-hand climbed off the morning train, and I sent him out to spread the word–'

'Yeah,' Clay said, exhaling, 'he came by the ranch.'

'First thing I did after finding the body,' Mays went on, 'was I woke Reid and told him to wire a message to the county sheriff. You know, Clay, the county might just as well station a deputy in Yellow Pine, what with all the trouble we've been having. It's that damned mining boom that did it, that's what caused our problems around here. I knew all along we were in for trouble–'

Tired of the storekeeper's relentless talk, Clay opened the back door and stepped outside, remembering Frenchy's account of this man's brief career as a town builder. He searched the ground behind the saloon, looked in the outhouse, then walked around the log building to the street.

Clay felt a numbing sense of loss, and anger. Frenchy was a good man, a trust-worthy man, and Clay had a sudden desire to know more about him. Where had he really come from? What was his background? With a great sadness, Clay realized that he would never know these things, and not even the man's real name.

Clay turned. Coming up the street from Cottonwood Creek was the waddling figure of Dirty Gertie. She wore a long dress of red velvet, a cowhand's brown boots with pointed toes, and on her head a wide-brimmed black hat topped with silk flowers.

'Mr Scarborough!' Gertie called out.

She made an odd, comic sight in the middle of the street, and Clay felt a weird compulsion to laugh – or cry. His emotions stormed as he watched the huge woman waddle toward him. By the time she reached him she was huffing like a steam engine at full throttle.

'Mr Scarborough,' Gertie said, gasping. 'I seen you ride past ... wanted to tell you ... had to get dressed...' She paused, taking several deep breaths. 'I seen him,' she said at last.

Clay immediately understood. 'The kid?'

Gertie nodded. 'That kid who was the wrangler for Mr Rawls. He stayed in my place all day yesterday, and most of last night. This morning when I woke up, he was gone.'

'You didn't see him leave?' Clay asked, louder than he intended.

Gertie shook her head, stirring oily hair

that had slipped out from under her flowered hat. 'He kept his mare tied behind my cabin all day… Sometime in the night he rode out.'

Clay turned and went to his horse. Jerking the reins from the rail, he swung up into the saddle. 'I'll go take a look,' he said, as he turned the gelding and rode away.

Trotting down the rutted street to Cottonwood Creek, Clay splashed across the shallow stream and guided his horse on to Dirty Gertie's cabin. He reined up, jumping out of the saddle before the horse stopped.

Clay rode around the cabin, finding the spot where Junior's mare had stood. Searching the ground around an empty water bucket, he found a few boot tracks in the soft dirt, along with some spilled oats.

At the Circle R, Clay thought ruefully, Junior had learned how to care for horses. The kid had planned ahead. The theft of food from Cookie's pantry made sense to Clay now. The kid hadn't left northern Montana at all. He'd camped out somewhere, hiding until the Circle R crew returned from Chicago. Then he'd ridden to Dirty Gertie's cabin.

Clay searched the grass in a widening circle until he found hoof prints leading away. Then he sprinted to his horse. The mare's tracks led northwest toward the Bear Paw mountains.

For the next three hours Clay followed his hunch more than the trail left by Junior's mare. To Clay's advantage, besides riding a stronger horse, was the fact that Junior had started his ride in darkness. Until daybreak the kid's progress would have been slow.

Seeing tracks here and there, and flattened grass where Junior had rested, Clay knew his hunch was right. The kid was headed for the north pasture.

Clay had to give him some credit. The plan was a good one. This time of year he was unlikely to meet any Circle R riders in the north sector of the ranch. Once through the north pasture, Junior could ride unseen to the base of Squaw Peak and follow the Old Blackfoot Indian trail over the pass, through the gold district, and on to its destination – Canada.

Shortly before noon Clay made another discovery as he trailed the kid's mare along the bank of a tributary to Cottonwood Creek. The hoof prints in the mud were un-usually small, and suddenly Clay remem-bered another time when he had seen tracks like these. The moment before he was shot last winter, he'd followed these hoof prints in the mud beside a creek.

CHAPTER 27

Clay spurred his horse on to the north pasture. He thought about Al Mays's remark that Frenchy had been beaten to death with 'something heavy, like a hammer or something.' That 'something' was very likely the butt of a heavy revolver, an old model Remington army revolver.

Riding the high ground, Clay looked ahead. On a bare stretch of earth he'd detected an unevenness in the mare's stride. She was tiring. The kid had pushed her too hard.

Crossing the last stretch of the north pasture that angled up to the granite-strewn slope, Clay saw a dark shape on the ground ahead. As he watched, the shape moved.

Clay drew his revolver and stood in the stirrups. Peering ahead into a low spot, he saw the mare lying in the grass. Junior had ridden her into the ground.

Approaching cautiously, Clay studied the rocky hill side. The kid was not there.

When Clay reached the low spot, he reined up beside the downed mare and dismounted. Holstering his gun, he bent down and took loose the saddle cinch. The mare raised her head and struggled, trying to regain her feet.

'Easy, girl,' Clay said, hearing her wheeze.

He swung into the saddle and rode to the base of the rocky slope, urging his horse ahead. As he rode upward through the sharp granite rocks, he remembered that almost exactly a year ago he'd led Curly and Wash and Junior up this same slope to the grassy flat at the base of Squaw Peak.

Steel horseshoes rang against stone as the gelding lunged on. At the top Clay felt the horse's sides heaving, but before he had a chance to look across the grassy flat, a shot was fired.

With a dull *thunk,* the bullet struck the gelding in the chest, dropping the big animal to its knees.

Clay spilled out of the saddle and rolled free as the horse toppled over. There was another shot and a bullet buzzed past Clay's ear like a lead hornet.

Scrambling to his knees, Clay dug his boots into the earth and leaped away, running for the stand of pine trees a hundred feet away.

Two more shots, quickly fired, missed. Clay dove behind a fallen tree, landing hard and scraping against dry branches. A third shot struck the tree.

Clay lay flat on the ground, breathing hard. A trickle of moisture ran down his cheek. He brushed a hand against his cheek, and brought away blood. A sharp branch

211

had slashed the side of his face.

Clay took off his hat. He rose on his elbows and peered through the branches of the pine tree. The grassy flat was littered with skeletons, the bare remains of steers and heifers that had been slaughtered by rustlers last year. Curving rib cages and horned skulls, weathered white as snow, lay on the ground. Behind one of them was Junior.

'Give it up!' Clay shouted.

Junior replied with another shot. The bullet slammed heavily into the fallen tree, shaking dried pine needles from the branches. Clay saw smoke drift up behind a rib cage amid tufts of grass.

The distance was too great for Clay's Colt .45. Junior's old Remington had greater range, Clay realized, and the kid could keep him pinned down here as long as his ammunition held out.

'Give it up!' Clay shouted again. 'A posse's coming!'

He hugged the ground as Junior fired two more shots. Clay wondered how many rounds the kid had. As freely as he was shooting, he probably had a box of fifty, plus a full cartridge belt.

Clay knew he had to do something to change their positions. Maybe he could make the kid do something foolish.

'Sam!' Clay shouted. 'Samuel Dillard!'

Clay heard a muffled cry of anguish, then came a blast of gunfire. Five shots slammed into the fallen tree. Clay hugged the ground.

Rising a few inches, he looked through the branches at the bleached rib cage and tufts of grass that concealed Junior.

'Why did you kill Frenchy?' Clay shouted. 'You could have tied him up and left him behind.'

'The little bastard didn't give me a chance!' Junior shouted back. 'He tried to kill me!'

'Like that rustler tried to kill you?' Clay asked. He was answered by silence. 'Like you bushwhacked me last winter?'

'Damn you, all I wanted was some cattle!' Junior fired four more shots in rapid succession.

These shots went wild, striking trees high overhead. The kid was losing patience, Clay realized. Then he saw movement behind the skeleton.

Junior sat up in full view, making a target of himself. He'd figured out that he was out of range of the Colt .45.

Clay shouted. 'You knew the combination to Frenchy's safe, didn't you? You were waiting for the right time to empty it out–'

'I knew everything but one number!' Junior shouted. 'One damned number! I had to beat it out of him!'

Clay had guessed that when the kid had first come to Yellow Pine and worked as a

213

swamper, he'd spied on Frenchy and managed to get the combination to the safe. The fact that the kid didn't know one of the numbers went a long way to explaining why he didn't want to leave northern Montana.

'Why did you shoot me?' Clay shouted.

'For all the times I shoveled manure instead of riding–' The kid's voice became anguished, and he snapped off two more shots. 'You ruined everything! You and that damned girl! The Old Man would have adopted me ... given me the Circle R...'

Clay thought he understood, twisted as the kid's reasoning was. In the beginning, Rawls might have said something about thinking of Junior as a son. With an idea of inheriting the ranch someday, Junior's fantasy must have come apart with Annie's arrival. He ran, after she'd rebuked him, with the idea of taking some cattle with him.

'When you came back last spring,' Clay shouted, 'you knew all along you'd rob the safe, didn't you?'

'Damn right!' Junior yelled. 'I fooled you, every one of you bastards!'

Everyone except Frenchy, Clay thought.

'Sam!' Clay shouted again, 'Sam Dillard! Give it up!'

With an anguished cry, Junior stood up behind the skeleton of the steer and fired three shots at Clay.

Clay pressed himself to the earth, feeling the tree shudder as two of the three bullets bit into the dry wood. He looked up and saw Junior reloading his revolver. Then the kid stooped down and picked up a pair of bulging saddlebags.

Clay watched as he slung the saddlebags over his shoulder, turned, and walked away. Rising on his elbows, Clay saw the kid striding toward the faint trail that led over Squaw Peak.

Clay scrambled to his feet. He leaped over the downed pine tree and sprinted into the open, pursuing the kid. Clay quickly closed the distance between them until Junior looked over his shoulder.

Junior stopped and let the saddlebags fall to the ground. He turned to face Clay, drawing his big revolver and taking deliberate aim.

Clay dove to the ground and rolled for the scant protection of a skeleton. He heard the roar of Junior's gun, and white shards of bone exploded into the air over him. Another shot, and the bullet *thunked* into the ground inches from his face.

Clay rolled again, out into the open. Even though he had no cover now, he knew that a moving target on open ground was better than a still one behind a skeleton.

Rolling to his stomach as Junior fired again, Clay brought his gun up, glimpsing the kid over his sights. Junior was striding toward him, holding the long-barreled revolver in front of him, taking dead aim at Clay.

Clay fired twice, raised the sights slightly, and fired twice more. Then he rolled away. A shot from Junior went wild, and when Clay came up again ready to shoot, he saw the kid sink to his knees and slowly crumble forward.

Clay watched the quivering body for several seconds, then got to his feet and ran to him. He kicked the Remington out of reach, and knelt beside Junior.

The kid's beardless cheek was pressed against the grass. His eye bulged open, as though straining against darkness. Clay saw that one of his bullets had taken the kid in the neck, just under the chin.

'Pa...' Junior whispered. 'Pa ... don't whip me...'

Clay saw his eye close. The kid's breath ran out, and he did not draw another.

CHAPTER 28

With the saddlebags slung over his shoulder, Clay made his way on foot down the rocky slope. When he reached the bottom, he found the mare. She had regained her feet, but stood with her legs spread wide, head drooping.

The mare was a ruined horse, but Clay was determined not to leave her for the wolves or a bear. He took the reins, tossed the saddlebags over her bare back, and led her out of the grassy hollow.

By sundown he had walked across the width of the north pasture to the creek. He stopped near the spot where he had established the new line camp this summer. Not far from here, on a grassy rise, were the graves of the two cowhands, Bill Clark and Zeb Hayes.

The mare drank from the stream after Clay slipped the bridle from her head. He knelt in the mud bank, splashed water over his face, then drank several handfuls of water. He moved back into the high grass beside the creek and lay on his back, looking up at the colorful sunset sky. A flood of memories came into his mind, memories of the past year.

Now it's over, he thought. Cattle have been shipped, Circle R herds are on their way to winter pasture, and the days are growing shorter and colder.

Hooves pounding on the earth came into his hearing, and Clay realized he had slept. The sky was pale and the light was thin now. He got up. The mare stood nearby, her ears cocked. Still hearing the horses, Clay saw no one.

He hesitated, then drew his revolver and fired it into the air. Holding the gun ready, he kept a watchful eye in the direction of the sounds of hoofbeats.

Presently two riders appeared over a rise a quarter of a mile away. As they drew closer, Clay recognized the square figure of Wash. Beside the big man rode Curly, a slender, small man moving smoothly with the gait of his loping horse.

'Clay!' Curly called out.

Clay waved, and holstered his gun.

'You all right?' Wash asked, riding up and halting his horse. Curly reined up beside him, looking from Clay to the mare and back again.

'I'm afoot,' Clay said. 'But I'm all right.'

'We've been after you since morning,' Curly said. 'Out on the range we crossed trails with a DHS rider on a Circle R horse. We stopped him and found out what happened. Me and Wash thought it over, and figured you'd be raising a posse. We high-tailed it for town. Al Mays told us that after you talked to Gertie, you lit out toward the mountains. We trailed you to find out what the hell's going on.'

Clay told them of his pursuit and confrontation with Junior.

'So he wanted to even the score with Frenchy,' Curly said, 'and hurt the Circle R, too.'

'That's right,' Clay said. He pointed to the saddlebags lying in the high grass. 'There's the money.'

Wash shook his head. 'Damned if that kid didn't leave a trail of killing behind him. I'm going to miss Frenchy.'

'I am, too,' Clay said. He picked up the saddlebags, and went to Curly's horse. 'I'll double up with you. Let's get home.'

In the following days the cash from Frenchy's safe was returned by the county sheriff as ranchers and cowhands brought their receipts to Yellow Pine. Frenchy was a meticulous bookkeeper, and when the last dollar was handed out, all receipts tallied with the books.

Clay sent a crew to the flat above the north pasture to recover Junior's body, along with Clay's saddle and bridle, and the saddle from the mare. The kid was buried a short distance away from the ranch house.

The evening after the burial Clay and Annie sat on the porch with the Old Man. Clay had never told him about Junior's real background, but the Old Man had heard the whole story from the county sheriff.

'I had that kid pegged wrong,' Rawls said now as the evening grew cool. 'I should have listened to you, Clay.'

After a long silence, Rawls went on. 'I know I'm getting cantankerous and forgetful...'

'Jess–' Clay said.

Rawls waved a gnarled hand in the air. 'No, it's the truth, Clay. That's why I've been in touch with my lawyer in Great Falls. I want to make some changes around here, and it's going to have to be put in writing, legal like.' He added, 'Those papers are going to be hand-delivered in a few days.'

'Papers?' Annie said.

Rawls looked at her, then at Clay. 'There's only one man I know who can hold this ranch together, and that's you, Clay. I'm making an offer to you. I'm offering you a full partnership in the Circle R, and when I die, this ranch goes to you and Annie. What do you say? Will you sign the papers?'

'That's an offer no man could turn down, Jess,' Clay said. 'Are you sure–'

'I'm still of sound mind, as the lawyer says,' Rawls interrupted. 'I know what I'm doing, besides giving you two a good reason to stay here.'

Clay looked at the smiling Annie, then said to the Old Man, 'I'll sign.'

Annie wrapped her arms around Clay. Inside the ranch house the baby began crying.

'Maybe someday,' Rawls said, his voice thick with emotion, 'you two will be handing the Circle R over to William Jess.'

'I reckon we will, Jess,' Clay said, grinning lopsidedly. 'I reckon we will.'

The publishers hope that this book has given you enjoyable reading. Large Print Books are especially designed to be as easy to see and hold as possible. If you wish a complete list of our books please ask at your local library or write directly to:

The Golden West Large Print Books
Magna House, Long Preston,
Skipton, North Yorkshire.
BD23 4ND

This Large Print Book, for people
who cannot read normal print,
is published under the auspices of

THE ULVERSCROFT FOUNDATION